The Secret Is

Kathleen Stauffer

Scripture references taken from the Holy Bible, Revised Standard Version, Thomas Nelson and Sons, New York, 1953

Scripture references taken from the Good News Testament, American Bible Society, 1976 (The New Testament in Today's English Version)

ISBN: 978-1-60383-322-6

Published by:
Holy Fire Publishing
717 Old Trolley Rd.
Attn: Suite 6, Publishing Unit #116
Summerville, SC 29485

www.ChristianPublish.com

Cover Design: Jay Cookingham

Printed in the United States of America and the United Kingdom

I dedicate this book to my mother
Marjorie June Shook Abel
1924-2009
…a person who
persevered
and loved unconditionally

Thank you, David, for being you.

luabc

All the wonders
You seek in life
Are deep inside
Yourself.

REFLECT

Hi, it's me Ledea. This was on a poster at our school. I memorized it because I think it's tied in with the secret. Hope you like my story.

Ledea

You've read those stories that begin, "Once upon a time…" The kind that usually end with, "They lived happily ever after." This is not that kind of story. Let me explain.

I knew from the beginning that I was different. I've never been able to put my finger on all the reasons; it's just a feeling I have. Not an alien or the beings you see in science fiction movies—that is not what I mean. Maybe I can help you understand.

I grew up with my mom, Mel, in a little town in the Midwest. I don't really know much about my dad. Mom said he named me Ledea because I was a girl, and Ledea sounded like lady. The nurses tried to tell my mom that Ledea should really be spelled L-y-d-i-a, but Mom said my dad had written it down as Ledea and that was that.

He was real excited the day I was born according to Mel but left town before my mom even came home from the hospital. Guess he had other plans. Mel was sure he loved me; however, since he had chosen such a pretty name. We have one picture of the three of us taken the day I was born. Mom keeps it in the bottom of her dresser drawer. About once a year, I would get it out—usually in the summer when I had more time. You can't see much of me—just a little nose placed on a red face inside a bunch of blankets. Mom looks tired and a little scared but is smiling down on me. Dad is smiling at the camera like a kid with a new toy. He didn't look like other dads.

Our house was in an area of town with no sidewalks, but we had lots of grass; Mel, my mom, called them weeds. In the winters after a snowstorm we stayed put until snowplows got to us—usually last because our end of town didn't seem to be as important.

The house Mel and I lived in was gray and small. A coat of paint would have improved it, but paint and brushes cost money. Besides the money, Mel didn't really have the time or the energy to undertake such a huge task.

Mel's parents lived towards the other end of town. They would help us out once in a while. Grandpa often seemed sick with coughing spells, and Grandma's arthritis made it difficult for her to get around. They would mumble to each other, a lot, mostly with their backs turned to each other in words I usually couldn't make out. Mel didn't go to their house much either. She said she was tired of their complaining about getting her butt in gear. Mel had a sister and brother in another state, but they never visited. I've seen pictures of them and their families in front of big houses or fancy cars like you see in commercials. We get one picture a year with a letter usually around Christmas time writing about things and places I don't know about. They look like some of the people of our very own town who wouldn't give me a smile or even a "hi" in passing.

Our neighbors lived in houses pretty much like ours. Some houses were empty with broken screens and critters crawling in and out. The neighbors pretty much kept to themselves. Having nothing else to do, I would watch from our window sometimes as they came home from work or shopping. Most minded their own business just like Mel and me. One family had four children who always seemed to have smudges on their faces and tears in their eyes; a lot of noise came from that house. Once I saw a woman with a briefcase leaving. She was dressed in a lady's suit and drove a car that said Department of Human Services on the side.

Mel went to work every day at a sock factory. She had to stand all day and used her hands a lot, so they were often sore. She talked about people from work, mostly someone named Ruthie and another person named Wilma. They worked side by side day in and day out, so I suppose if Mel had friends, it would've been Ruthie and Wilma.

I guess she liked her job. She said it was a good paying job for her with no high school education plus we had benefits. Mel seemed to understand the benefits thing, but she never explained it to me.

Mel told me she had failed every test she had ever taken in school and still remembers getting papers with big, red-inked F's on the top. When it came to parent-teacher conference time for me, she usually skipped. When the special education meeting time rolled around, she would tell the school she was sick, but they made her go. She was uncomfortable with the whole idea of having to set foot in a place she hated while she was growing up. Anyway, she quit school sometime in high school. I guess they didn't miss her much. Mel said she got the flu in the winter one year. After three days out of school, she figured life was a lot less stressful staying home even with Grandpa and Grandma mumbling about not amounting to much. The school called only once to check on her whereabouts, according to Mel.

With Mel at work and me at school or doing house chores in the summer, our life was pretty boring. Not much ever happened. We had money for food at the local Red Owl and new clothes from the Dollar Store once in a while. We had no car to take us to other places. Mel had never tried to get her driver's license; instead, she rode an old bike everywhere. It had a basket so she could take her lunch to work or carry home a small bag of groceries. Once after a bad winter storm, Ruthie from work picked Mel up and brought her home. Otherwise, except for a rare trip with Grandpa and Grandma, the bike or our feet was our way of getting around.

Sunday was the special day of the week. A *day of rest* I heard somewhere. Mel and I would attend church every Sunday when I was little. We never missed. Up until the 8th grade, I attended Sunday School. Mel would walk with me to the church, drop me off at my room and then sit in the main part of the church until Sunday School was out so we could go to church together. Church mostly made me feel warm and fuzzy inside. We always wore our best clothes and sometimes stayed for donuts and coffee afterwards. People would say things like, "Nice day isn't it?" and "Good to see you this morning."

I say *mostly* warm and fuzzy because there were two times I remember that I felt like a non-member of the human race at church. One time happened at children's sermon. Pastor Simmons had all the kids come up front for a little talk. We sat at his feet. On this particular Sunday, everywhere I tried to sit, a foot or hand would be stuck out to cover the spot. When I finally found an empty spot, two girls nearby made funny faces to each other, pinched their noses shut with their thumbs and pointer fingers and moved away from me like I had fleas. It was enough for me to plan not to come up to children's sermon again. However, Pastor Simmons, with his wise and kind eyes, focused on me that day when he talked of Jesus' love. In my heart I knew that I was truly loved by Jesus if not by others. I wanted to hear more of these words, God's words, as Pastor Simmons called them.

The other time I felt unwanted at church was really more embarrassing. I went to use the girl's restroom after Sunday School. The custodian with her beady eyes seemed to be guarding it with her very life that day. After using the toilet, I flushed and opened the stall door to see her standing before me with sponge and spray bottle in hand. She looked at me and said, "I'll really have to scrub now." She started with the spray almost before I could leave the stall. She must have thought I had leprosy—something awful someone had in a Bible story we studied. After that day, I planned my Sunday mornings so I would not be using the restroom.

School was difficult for me. Church, however, was pure pleasure. I could sit and listen to Pastor Simmons' sermons as if the words were fairy dust being sprinkled over Mel and me. I did not always understand the words, and the ones I thought I did understand, I realize now probably had different meanings for me than they did for others.

I memorized my favorite verses from the Bible. I would bring the bulletins home and place them under my pillow. Each night I would read the favorite verse over and over until it was set in my mind. There is one from Hebrews I said to myself when I felt like someone was treating me in a way which made me feel scummy or bad about myself. It goes, "The Lord is my helper. I will not be afraid. What can man do to me?" Repeating it until I felt strong again, "What can man do to me?" made me feel like I could take just about anything and survive because Jesus was truly my helper and on my side. I simply had to love and trust him.

Another verse came from Deut.--I'm not sure how you spell the whole thing. "The eternal God is your dwelling place and underneath are the everlasting arms." When I felt lonely, I would see myself living with God and his everlasting arms holding me. This was really a pretty simple picture: me and God. I did, however, have trouble memorizing it as I would turn around everlasting and eternal. I know enough about words to know that this was probably ok as they both meant about the same thing.

There's two more I want to share. Sorry. Proverbs 25:11 reads, "A word fitly spoken is like apples of gold in pictures of silver." When Pastor Simmons first spoke these words they sounded like music. I didn't know the meaning and even stopped listening to the rest of his sermon as I searched the bulletin to re-read them. It took weeks to get this verse set in my head. I kept confusing apples and silver and pictures and gold, mixing them up and turning them around. After finally getting it down, I would say it to myself when I wanted to feel intelligent. Even though I was a special ed. student, I'm good with words. My teacher told me that the language section of my Test of Basic Skills was just as good as that of a lot of kids in regular education. Anyway, these words sounded light and musical, and I could imagine the golden apples in silver pictures and how beautiful a sight this could be.

The other verse which really begins this whole story is about a **secret**. It's in Colossians. You can look it up in your Bible if you like. It's in the first chapter and verse 27. It reads: *God's plan is to make known his secret to his people, this rich and glorious secret which he has for all people.* **And the secret is that Christ is in you...** Now, everyone loves secrets. That's why I first memorized it. However, as the years have passed, the **secret** opened my eyes to many things. Some of them, quite profound. (There's another word you could look up—profound— you'll need the dictionary for this one.)

When I was 17 and attending what they call a special school, a bus took me and a few others to our worksites and other places we needed to go. The word *special* on buses or above classrooms always strikes me as funny. Actually, depending on the day, I didn't know whether to giggle or cry. What's special about us? If we're special, why do others make fun of us?

Mrs. Stenzel, the teacher who spent most of the time with me, thought it was important that we understood our disabilities. Some people called us retards or retarded, but Mrs. Stenzel said that term had a stigma and wasn't appropriate. Stigma sounded like sting to me. I looked it up. The definition was confusing, but I remember thinking that *sting* was as good a definition as the dictionary's.

Mrs. Stenzel tried to explain our disabilities but said we needed to concentrate on our strengths. We should be aware of our weaknesses so we could learn coping or managing skills. She believed that everyone had a weakness, but not everyone's weakness was educationally significant. For example, if you are born without any toes, it will affect your balance, but you could still be a star math student. Or, maybe you were born with a heart defect of some kind, but you could still read over 100 words a minute. How's that for an explanation? I guess most people are luckier than I was because my weakness or disability made me feel stupid. Mel told me they had to put a shunt in my brain after I was born and that's why learning was hard for me. It's a headache in more than one way. Joke—get it?

Mrs. Stenzel drew a dough boy on the blackboard one day and put a small circle on one side of his body. "Think of your disability as that dot," she explained. "That is only one part of you. The rest of you is like everybody else." It made me feel better, this explanation, at least for a short time.

In our classroom, we had ten students. Although we're not supposed to use labels, I knew that Mattie and Sal had behavior disorders. The rest of our class had learning disabilities or mental disabilities. Ward had really thick glasses and walked funny. His shoes were way too big; I hope that's not the reason why he walked the way he did. It's not like we looked a lot different than any other kid in school, but because we learned differently, some students treated us differently.

Like I said, Mrs. Stenzel wanted us to understand our disabilities and each other. She read a book to us one day. It was especially for kids with learning disabilities. It was called, *What is L.D. and Why Am I L.D.?* According to the book, the kids with L.D. are of average intelligence but have trouble with one area or two like reading or math. Mrs. Stenzel stated that we should think of L.D. as "learning differently" rather than "learning disabled." I came up with my own: "Learning is Difficult." The part on *why* we were this way was mainly confusing to me. I think it had something to do with brain damage or something that might have happened when we were born.

Mrs. Stenzel said she had checked to see if a similar book was available for those with a mental disability, like M.D., but there was not. She recommended to the book company that they print one.

What it comes down to is that we all went to this special part of the school because Learning is Difficult

(L.D.). Most of the time, we felt pretty good about ourselves. However, some of the time, we just felt stupid. I sometimes think about this when I pull that picture of my so-called family out taken on the day I was born. I knew Mel had trouble in school; did my dad even go?

Everyone does stupid things off and on during a lifetime, but to feel stupid a lot is not a good feeling. I used to think stupidity and ignorance were the same. Remember, I told you I was good with words. Anyway, we used to pass this English teacher on the way to the bus each day, and he would smile and say, "Ignorance is bliss." I asked Mrs. Stenzel about it, and she said that Mr. Gray was just preparing himself for his next class and to pay no mind.

Mrs. Stenzel did a lot to try to help make us feel smart and good about ourselves. We covered self-advocacy strategies so that we could ask for what we needed and wanted and do it in a successful way. We had to memorize this explanation word for word. We covered problem-solving strategies to use with our friends, at home, and on work sites. All of our math was life functioning math. We would have had a tough time with stuff other students called algebra and geometry. I never did understand who started putting letters with numbers in the first place. To me, it's mixing things that shouldn't be mixed—like putting mashed potatoes with chocolate chip cookies. Eaten separately, they're ok. Mixed together—you get the picture?

Back to our classroom. When I think of the Bible verse about the secret, that Christ is in me, I know it must apply to everyone who believes. But, what about those who don't, or aren't sure, or haven't had a chance to believe? More about this later. I can believe Christ is within Mrs. Stenzel as she was so kind and caring. I had a little more trouble with believing Christ was in people like Mattie and Sal as there were times when they made life so miserable. Although, if you talk about the truth— Mattie and Sal would not have chosen to be the way they were.

They both had behavior management plans. They got points for behaving a certain way and points taken away when they lost it. When I say "lost it," I'm not talking about things that are lost. Some pretty strange things happened in our room, and I can honestly say that during those times, I felt fortunate to be a kid with a learning disability instead of the terrible curse Mattie and Sal must have had inside them.

Mattie was really calm most of the time, but when he started to lose it, and there never seemed to be a really good reason why he lost it, we knew the class was in for a half a day of being really careful around Mattie. He usually started by taking his desk apart and drawing obscene pictures on it or his chair. I looked closely after the principal had come to get Mattie one day. With black marker, Mattie had drawn a devil holding a knife with blood dripping from the knife. Sometimes, he would throw things or simply walk out of the room. All the kids in regular ed. did their best to stay away from him but didn't help by saying things like *psycho-boy* beneath their breath—not loud enough to get themselves into trouble but loud enough for Mattie to hear.

Sal was just as scary in a different way. Life just got to her. It could have been extra noise, someone disagreeing with her, a red check mark on her work, or someone forgetting to say hi to her. One day the cops had to pick her up as she was yelling curse words at students in the hall while throwing things from her locker. We all felt a little sick that day because she was one of us from the special ed. room. People sometimes put us all in the same pot, thinking we're all alike, and we were not.

The other kids in our classroom pretty much minded their own business. They did their school work and tried to make it good on their work-sites. The work-sites were part of our school day, and we even got credit for them like you do with a class.

In October of our junior year, a new student came to our room. Maria had moved to our town from somewhere in Louisiana. She was so shy the first couple of weeks that when someone looked at her, she would blush and hide her face in her hands. I thought she was hopeless. She started choosing me as a partner for some of our work--probably thinking I was the least scary of the others in our classroom. Eventually, we became friends.

Maria was darker skinned than me with thick, brown hair that covered a lot of her face. She might have been pretty except her face parts were kind of large. I'm quiet like Maria, but I'm pasty-white and skinny with blonde, fly-away hair. I wear glasses I have to push up all the time. Mel said that if my nose weren't so flat, I wouldn't have to do that. Anyway, Maria and I became good friends. We would even write F/F at the bottom of our notes to each other. If you don't know what F/F means—it's Friends Forever.

Maria couldn't read very fast or do math word problems; however, the math facts, she had them down. I felt smart around Maria, but I still respected her because she treated me like a best friend, and I hadn't had many in my life.

After school we started walking home together. Soon, summer came and Maria and I started spending a little time together each day usually watching the soaps. As the days passed, Maria and I shared secrets I had never shared with anyone. Like the time this regular ed. kid, named Chris, said he wanted to marry me. All of his friends laughed when he said it, but I think about it to this day wondering why he said it. Even if it meant he liked me just a little, it made me feel really good. After that day when I saw him in the hall, his friends would sometimes push him towards me, saying, "C'mon, Chris, ask her." He would yell back to cut it out or worse words. I'm not sure what it all meant.

Maria said that when she lived in Louisiana, kids treated her worse. They teased her about never washing her hair and the kind of clothes she wore. She was even called retard on the playground and was the last one chosen for any games. She missed some things about her old home but felt that her new school was better.

Maria's home was not like mine. I could believe the secret about Maria. She was gentle, sweet and kind and would hurt no one. But her family was not like her or Mel or me. She lived just three blocks from me. Two large, barking dogs on chains killed anything green that had been growing in their front yard. No need to mow at their house. The house was small like ours, except six people lived there. It had a tiny living room, a tiny kitchen and two bedrooms. The bathroom was in a corner of the kitchen with a blanket blocking the view. I hate to talk about the smell, but it's hard not to, because it was always there from the minute you walked in: greasy food, sweat, and the smell you get when you haven't cleaned the bathroom for a year or two. Maria sometimes complained about how small and crowded her house was, but the smell didn't seem to bother her. Sometimes, she even smelled like her home, and I didn't know how to tell her without hurting her feelings.

Mel and I got along pretty good. I guess with just two of us and that being all we had, we were naturally close. Maria's family was at war most of the time. Her brothers used bad language and never minded anyone with the exception of Maria's dad who would threaten them with a beating. Maria's mom and dad fought, too, using words that were new to me. I wondered how a family could ever survive with them all acting so hateful to each other. Maria wasn't a big mouth like her brothers. She did her chores, didn't talk back, but her mom and dad still yelled at her. It's like it was behavior that was programmed in them. They opened their mouths; bad words came out.

Maria dreamed of going away and having a place of her own someday. Her dad, however, told her she was dumb, could never hold down a job, and a bunch of other worse things having to do with boys. Worst of it, she believed him. It puzzled me that Mrs. Stenzel could talk to us every day about our strengths and how we could use our strengths to become independent in the adult world, and then somebody like Maria's dad could kill all that good with his nasty words.

In August, about two weeks before school started, Maria and I were out walking the streets because it was too hot to be inside. It wasn't time for either of us to be home. We talked about who would be in our classroom next year and how we'd have to miss out on the soaps until next summer and what might happen in the meantime. It was about ten p.m. We were about to separate when we heard this car coming down the street real slow. When it got right beside us, it stopped. Maria immediately covered her face with her hands. I thought about running, but I knew Maria would just stand there like a dummy. Someone from the car spoke my name, so I looked. I recognized some kids from our high school. The only one I knew by name was Chris.

"Wanna go for a ride?" one of them yelled.

I looked around for help. The streets were empty except for us and this car.

"We need to get home," I answered like a weakling.

"Oh, come on. Just down the road and back."

"No," I managed to say in a squeaky, loud voice. My heart started to hurt because it was beating too fast.

"C'mon, Ledea, do it for me." It was Chris. Maybe he really did like me.

I turned to Maria. All I could see was all that brown hair and her hands still covering her face. She was bent over at the waist with her hair hanging down to her knees.

Trying to pull one of her arms from her face, I asked, "What do you think?"

Her shape shrugged.

I turned back to the car. "Well, I guess…"

The car door opened, and we climbed in with three others already in the backseat. Three more were in the front. I smelled smoke and something else sweet and sour on their breath. It was hot, muggy and uncomfortable. Everyone seemed to be touching everyone else; it was crowded. I wanted out as soon as I got in, but the door slammed shut.

The talk sounded fuzzy. They acted different than they did in school. Chris was in front sitting in the middle beside some guy with long, stringy hair. I noticed his dark, dark eyes whenever he turned around to look at me. He had a scary look; or, was it worried? I kept my eyes on the back of Chris' head trying to make myself feel better about all of this. Maria was stuffed beside me with her face still in her hands. With a squeal of tires we sped off. The boys offered us cigarettes and something to drink. There was a lot of kidding around about stuff I didn't understand. Before long we were in the country and on gravel roads.

Someone next to me whispered in my ear. I couldn't understand it, but I could feel something warm and sticky. Soon his hands were under my shirt touching places I'd never touched. My armpits and palms became prickly, and the pit of my stomach felt sick. I clutched Maria's arm and said, "We gotta get out of here." I didn't care who heard me.

"You ain't goin' no where," the guy with his hands under my shirt said.

The car seemed to be going faster and faster. Trees were a dark blur alongside the road. Maria, sounding like a lost kitten, cried next to me. I'm sorry now, but all I could think of was "dummy." I was mad at Maria for acting so helpless. And, I was mad at myself.

Someone turned the radio on so loud the car shook. I covered my ears as Maria grabbed my arm and buried her wet face in it. The guy next to me put his hand on my bare knee and cursed when I shoved it away. Placing a hand over my heart to try to settle it, I starting saying over and over, "The Lord is my helper, I will not be afraid, what can man do to me? The Lord is my helper…" But, at the same time, I was thinking that if there was a hell, we were on our way there. The car hit some loose gravel and went out of control. We rolled over and over and over. Arms and legs were flying. I heard the sound of screams, moans, glass breaking, and metal cracking. Then, silence. Silence. I could smell sweaty bodies, hot wires, and something new—blood.

Cool air fell on my right cheek and I turned to see a broken-out window. Carefully, I untangled my arms and legs and crawled out. Once outside the car, the night seemed deadly still. Voices packed with pain soon filled all the empty dark spaces around me. Some were coming from inside the car; some from the grass in the ditch we landed in. Someone weakly said, "Help." Another voice moaned, "Oh, God." Someone else mumbled, "Jesus Christ."

"Maria!" I screamed. No answer. I tried to look for her, but there was so much darkness and my glasses were gone. I crawled out of the ditch and noticed a light down the road and took off running. A wet, sticky feeling on my right leg and a sick feeling in my stomach made me want to stop, but knew I could not. The kids in the car were badly hurt. I had to get help.

There was a light inside the farmhouse. More scared than I had ever been in my life, I beat at the door, yelling, "Help, help me, please!" It was only a few moments before the door opened slowly to show a heavy man in striped over-alls.

"What do you want, girl?" He was rubbing the whiskers on his chin and looking behind him like there was someone else in the house with him.

"There's been an accident. A bad accident! We need help. Please call someone!"

He stood there and studied me. All I could think of was that people were dying, and this man was trying to figure something else out.

"Where you from girl?"

"Town. Please, call the ambulance!"

I was sweaty and hurt and terrified. However, the look I was getting was not one of understanding but rather a look of being puzzled. My somewhat heavy lidded eyes, flat nose and pinched mouth were strange to him. I think he mistrusted me. During this very bad moment, my mind flashed back to the time Ruthie had given my mom a ride home from work that winter day when the storm was too awful for Mel to be walking. Ruthie came in and during a short visit, Mel got out our family picture. You know, the one taken the day I was born. The one with me and Mel and the dad I never knew. Ruthie's eyes grew wide and her eyebrows went up.

"He looks like someone who crawled out from under a rock," she laughed.

Mel laughed, too, sort of.

"Please, sir, it's down the road. The accident. That way." I pointed in the direction I had come from.

"You go on back to your friends. I'll call." And he closed the door with a thudding sound.

I felt more alone than I had ever felt in my life. I didn't know which direction town was. I only knew the accident was back down the road and that my friend, Maria, needed help.

I don't remember much else about that night except that soon there were other cars, the police, an ambulance, and talk of death. Mel was soon at my side, and I recognized Maria's parents somewhere with the others in what must have been an emergency room. There were people with light blue masks over their lower faces, tubes hooked to machines and a funny smell of medicine.

Sharp words were spoken by someone dressed in clothes I've seen in catalogs.

"Who's responsible for this? I want to know, now!" he demanded.

When this loud man passed my cot with my mom at my side, I heard him ask a nurse, "She was with them?"

He said *she* like a curse word. Tears formed in my eyes but I could not cry. I remember thinking, "What can man do to me?" and answering myself, "Man is killing my very soul."

Mornings, afternoons, evenings. I was not aware of time. There was a needle stuck in my arm and a lot of pain. I remember having to go inside a machine like a tunnel for a test. No machine could see what was really inside me. Even though deep in sadness and hurting, I believed God's love was there, too, and that he would help me through this.

I started school that fall at the end of October. Maria did not. You see, not only is Christ in Maria because of her sweet, gentle spirit; but Christ is also beside Maria. Maria's not living down the street. Maria is not choosing me for her partner in our class. Maria is in heaven. At least, Pastor Simmons has told me so.

One of Chris' friends also died in the accident. He was a guy by the name of Rick Jackson. He was to be a senior. There was a special get-together for him at our high school before school started. I was still hospitalized, but I heard there was a lot of crying and speeches by other students. Maria would have graduated from the same class, but I didn't hear of anything special for her. I've often wondered about that—here she was in special education but not *special* enough to be honored in death. I'm glad God doesn't work that way.

On some days I see Chris when I'm getting on the bus headed for my worksite. He's driving up in a small sports car. He doesn't look as happy as he used to. Maybe Rick Jackson was a close friend of his. Maybe not. I'll never know. Maybe he's got other things on his mind—like college or that new girl friend I've seen him with. She was a cheerleader and had these white teeth that show up all the way down the hallway. Everyone says hi to her—most everyone.

When I was hospitalized, Mel visited me every day. Mrs. Stenzel stopped in after school a couple of times a week. Pastor Simmons visited me often at the hospital and even after I came home, he would come to our house. Pastor Simmons surely has Christ in him. I think Mel does, too, but maybe she doesn't know it the way I understand it.

Since the accident, I've been doing a lot of thinking about things I had not really thought about before. There are so many unanswered questions. Why is it ok to be friends with some people but not with others? What is hate? Why are people afraid of one another? Are fear and hate possibly the same?

If God breathed into Adam the breath of life so that Adam could live, and if Adam was the first man, the first father—then, we all truly do have Christ within us. So, is he just buried in some of us? Is he there, but not showing? I know I have limitations, but some things I can put together. It seems to me there are no good answers to some questions. Maybe this is part of the *human nature* thing Pastor Simmons mentions now and then.

I graduated in the spring. Mrs. Stenzel talked about transition plans and would we be ready for community life? My worksite was at the local Red Owl grocery store. I started out washing dishes but soon learned how to broast the chicken and use the deli meat slicer. They've offered me a job for the summer saying *We'll see how it goes....* Minimum wage. Also, with the help of Mrs. Stenzel, I passed the written part of my driving license test. There's no car parked in front of our house with my name on it, but I feel like everyone else having the driver's license card with my picture right on it in my purse. Mrs. Stenzel said it would be a good thing to have for identification.

Some dreams that refused to come to me had to do with family. I knew that Mel would not be with me forever. People grow old and die. It's a fact of life. I heard something once about death and taxes but am not sure how it fits. Anyway, without Mel, who would I live with? Could I live on my own? Who would I spend time with? Mattie, you remember from our class? He asked me out every week of our senior year. But, what kind of life could Mattie give me with his set of problems? He probably would have ended up yelling curse words to me when he got mad, just like Maria's dad did to her mom. I still thought of Chris, but in my heart I knew Chris, or anyone like him, was as far away as the moon and stars. No one like him could ever be a part of my life.

Mel and I still attended church most Sundays. I thought about putting my favorite Bible verses in a book. The title would have simply been, *Ledea's Favorite Verses*, by Ledea Jenkens. Of course, I didn't write them. God did. Later, I took to memorizing hymns. I decided to memorize *Blessed Assurance* because I liked the verse, "This is my story, this is my song…." It was easy to understand, even the stuff about praise. I knew I was happier if I could just remember to praise God for the good stuff and try not to dwell on the bad.

However, the interesting stuff started to happen when I decided to memorize the main part. It started out with, "Blessed assurance, Jesus is mine…" Yes, I thought, Jesus is mine; He's within me and all others who believe. The "heir of salvation; purchase of God" was a little confusing. Mel said it had something to do with eternal life and heaven. "Born in his spirit, washed in his blood" goes back to the secret—again! We are actually *born* in his spirit! And the washed-in-his-blood has to do with dying on the cross and Easter; he paid the price so our sins could be forgiven. It's all so connected.

Whenever we sung "Blessed Assurance" in church, I almost couldn't. This big lump would form right in my throat and the tears would come. So, I would hum it during church and sing the words to myself after getting in bed sometimes soaking my pillow with the tears. It's kind of amazing how the things you learn when you're growing up—a lot of it sticks with you for life.

You could think of this first chapter as kind of an autobiography of part of my growing up years. Some good. Some not so good. Stay with me. You're about to meet Star. There's no one like him. Some good. Some not so good.

Star

I first saw Star when working at the Red Owl—my first job. I worked in the deli dishing out chicken and potatoes with gravy available most every day, meatloaf on Mondays, tater tot casserole on Tuesdays, etc. They had a special every day. Anyway, Star loved the Red Owl broasted chicken.

"Dark meat. It's what I want and lots of gravy. Keeps my joints lose," he almost shouted like he wanted everyone to know he was there ordering his chicken. A person couldn't miss him if a person wanted to. Star always wore the same thing: black cowboy boots, tight black jeans, a black shirt with pearl buttons and a black cowboy hat. Someone asked him once if he had any other clothes. He studied them a bit and then grinned.

"Looks good on me, right? If it ain't broke, don't fix it."

I would have guessed Star to be around 30 when he started coming to the Red Owl.   I was quiet and didn't say much to the other workers, but I overheard quite a bit. The ladies were almost embarrassed around him; I think it had something to do with his tight pants— they even said as much. The carry out boys, high schoolers, made fun of him. I think it was because Star was like no one they had ever known. No one seemed to know where he came from or why he started coming to the Red Owl on a regular basis.

"Just a drifter," our deli manager said one day. "They come and go, find a job for while, earn a little cash, and then they're gone."

I would have not paid much attention to Star. I guess you could say that he started it. He started asking for me to get his chicken dinners. Like making a request. I couldn't believe my own ears when he first asked for me.

"Who's that skinny gal with the long, blonde hair. I'll have her wait on me, today."   Everyone pushed me toward the counter giggling the entire time causing me to bump the container holding the broasted chicken.   I winced and grabbed the palm of my hand.

"What's the matter, hon-ey?" His eyes twinkled.

"Nothing. It's nothing. Can I help you?" I didn't know whether to be mad, embarrassed or feel special.

"Dark meat. Lots of gravy. Keeps the joints lose." He grinned the whole time I dished up the potatoes and gravy and chicken. I wiped off the extra gravy that had dribbled over the side with my apron leaving a brown, greasy stain on the side of the box.

"Wanna join me?" He winked.

I was not good with the quick come-back. So, I looked away quickly and said nothing. Even though my hand was shaking, I wrote the price of the chicken special on his styro foam box with a black marker, handed it to him, and turned to wait on another customer.

"A bit shy, isn't she?" He announced to the entire deli department who were in some kind of trance by this time. Probably dumb-founded thinking, Star's *paying attention to Ledea?* Star's attention to me made me nervous. Why was he picking on me?

After the first couple of times, everyone knew that when Star came in, I was supposed to wait on him. I guess you could say I started looking forward to it even though the shaking didn't stop for some time. Like I said earlier, he was a lot older than I was by 10 years or so, but he always treated me politely and called me hon-ey with the "hon" drawn way out before he said the "eee".

He didn't ask if I wanted to join him, for the dinner, that is, for a long time. He told me later that he figured he was scaring me away. Instead, I would hand him the chicken dinner. He would say, "Thank you, very much." After several weeks I started answering with, "Thank *you* very much." If you knew me, you would understand how quite forward it was for me to talk like that. I felt like I was flirting. And, that's how our relationship started.

Soon, Star came not only on the chicken special days but other days as well. He said the Red Owl deli was the best place to get a good meal in town. Once, I had my break soon after Star paid for his meal. I walked out the automatic doors, went to the large window facing the parking lot and saw him sitting there in his truck eating all by himself. Someplace inside me felt sorry for him. He acted so important and there he was all by himself—having no one to eat with.

After that, I started wishing that Star *would* ask me to eat with him. Not having the courage to ask him, I would linger a little longer after his order. One day, I tried some conversation.

"What's it like outside?" I murmured, surprising myself.

"What's that, hon-ey?" Star almost did a double-take—me speaking and all.

"What's it like outside?" My throat kind of hurt. I wasn't used to talking that loud.

"Well, it's not rainin' cats and dogs, that's for sure," and his eyes got big like it was Christmas or something. "Why do you want to know?"

"Just wondered." Me, murmuring, again.

"What?" Star leaned his ear toward me.

"Just wondered!" This time my throat did hurt.

"Oh." That seemed to stump him—me, just wondering.

"Wanna go on a picnic?" He asked staring at me wide-eyed.

I stared back.

"Cat got your tongue?" He smiled and finally blinked.

"Noooo," I wasn't smiling. What was this stuff about a cat and my tongue?

"Well, what do you think? Picnic or not?" Star's voice kept getting louder with each question he asked.

Now, there's something I haven't told you about Star. And, that is the fact that he talked differently than anyone else I had ever known. I mentioned earlier in the "Ledea Chapter" that I was always good with English in school. Stuff like spelling, grammar, and vocabulary were easy for me. Some regular education kids were even puzzled by the fact that I could know this stuff better than them.

But Star apparently had a different education than I did because he used all these expressions that I didn't understand. Like *rainin' cats and dogs, if it ain't broke don't fix it, and cat got your tongue.* Not wanting to ask stupid questions, I just pretended that the words didn't make a difference. Although I admit that as time passed, I didn't know if he was being sweet or trying to hurt me on purpose. More on that later.

"Picnic," I answered.

"Picnic?" I could tell I had surprised him, but right away he kept babbling with, "Hokie, dokie, hon-ey, when?" like he was afraid I'd change my mind if he didn't keep making the plans.

"When?" I was starting to blush. Others were listening. "I don't know." This was going to be harder than I thought.

"Well, hon-ey, when do you get off work tomorrow?" He had his hands in his pockets and was shifting his feet.

"One o'clock. After the noon rush." I kept my eyes on his black boots.

"That's it. Picnic tomorrow. My treat."

I turned to go to the back room to wash my hands and ran into two old ladies who worked with me. Snooping they were. They said, "Whoops, whoops, excuse me," but I knew why they were so close—hanging on every word, they were.

I walked home that day with mixed feelings. Going from feeling happy to feeling scared to feeling funny—in a weird way. Mel asked me how the day had gone. Ok. I asked her. Ok. And, we watched TV like we do every night. I had never had a date before. I didn't know how Mel would react. And, would Star even show up? The way he was shifting his feet got me worried a little. That night I couldn't sleep. Would we eat in his truck? Would he take me to the park? What if Mel saw me riding around in his pickup? What would we talk about?

I had a headache when I got up in the morning and my jaw hurt. I took a shower, put on a little lipstick and tried to do something with my wispy hair. Looking in the mirror, my lips looked funny with all that color, so I washed it off. Pulling my hair back in a pony tail, I slipped my cotton work apron over my t-shirt and headed to work.

Shaping rolls, baking, frosting, slicing meat, making sandwiches, the minutes seemed to pass ever so slowly. If I would have had Star's number, I would have called him and told him I was sick. The whole thought of this was beginning to make me feel like puking. During the night, my mind kept drifting back to the car accident from high school and what those boys were up to or would've been had we not had the awful wreck. Would Star be like that? And then I would talk myself out of it, telling myself it was during the day—no problem.

So, you see how it went. Back and forth in my brain all morning. It's no wonder I had a splitting headache when Star showed up early at 12:30. When I saw him walk in the Red Owl, I panicked. My heart started the thump-thump thing it does when I feel frightened. Star eyed me at the deli as if to make sure I was there, and then wandered about the store pushing a cart as if he had groceries to buy. I had never seen him buy anything other than food from the deli, so I found this interesting how he could waste a half hour pushing an empty cart around the Red Owl.

At 12:50, he approached the deli and ordered.

"Chicken for two. Dark meat. Lots of gravy." My hands shook as I dished up the potatoes and gravy. Star wasn't being his usual noisy loud self.

"You do like dark meat?" He asked me in a very polite voice.

"Sure."

I handed him the two dinners.

"Meet you outside the door?" He questioned.

"Sure. In a minute."

I think if there had been an escape route, I would have taken it. However, the only backdoors available were for delivery trucks. Everyone who worked at the grocery store would have known what I did. It would be the talk for weeks. I knew I had to go. Timing out, taking off my apron, and grabbing my purse, everyone of my co-workers told me goodbye. Everyone! Anyone shopping in the store would have thought it was a going-away party for Ledea or something like that.

"Enjoy that chicken, Ledea," one of the deli workers said and winked at me.

"Have a good time on that picnic," another said.

"We'll miss you," one of the snoopy old ladies said with a giggle.

I could tell you detail by detail what happened at the picnic, but you would find it boring. To sum it up, I survived. Star drove us to the city park; we sat at a picnic table and ate. We were both hungry which is a good thing because even Star didn't have a lot to say. I was beginning to wonder if he had wished I had said no. He looked at his watch, said, "time flies," and started gathering our used paper plates and napkins. After dumping them in a nearby trash can, we headed back to the pickup where he opened the door for me. It creaked. He slammed the door shut after I got in and stood at the rolled-down window.

"Ain't got no bells and whistles, but it's steady," he looked deep into my eyes. I didn't know what bells and whistles he was talking about, so I stared back.

"Ledea, you look like you got a bee in your bonnet. Penny for your thoughts." He was looking at me, of course, because he was talking to me. I was looking at him because he was too close to ignore and because I could think of nothing to say back to him with all that nonsense talk he always used.

During this time, I noticed his dark whiskered face; dark, thick eyebrows; and large pupils. A few sweat beads ran down the side of his face. I didn't do this on purpose, but my eyes kind of shifted down his face to his lips. Chicken grease; it's what I saw. He closed his eyes and his lips were puckered. I turned my face just in time to get a quick kiss on my right cheek. My first reaction was to wipe it off. Instead, I brought my right hand down and placed it on my lap inside my left hand. Meanwhile, Star was walking behind the pickup and getting into his side--the whole time whistling. As he plopped himself in, I noticed the smile on his face—like he had gotten by with something.

As he turned the key, he stated matter-of- factly, "Ledea, we're birds of a feather. You know what that means?"

I finally had a chance to say something. "No."

"Well, I'm not ready to jump off the deep-end yet, but I think we should do this, again, sometime. Are you ok with that?"

"Yes." I kept looking at my hands wanting to touch my face where he had kissed.

Our once a week date continued for about two months. It was always chicken. It was always at the park. Someone at work said, "He's gettin' too big for his britches," and then would smile and squeeze her eyes shut. I remember this particular comment because others said it a lot. It seemed to me they were starting to talk more like Star. Other comments included things like *pulling the wool over your eyes* and *pulling your leg*. I didn't know what all this pulling meant, but everyone was kind and considerate, so I let it go.

One afternoon at the park after licking the chicken grease off our fingers, Star said he needed to get serious. Thinking I had done something wrong, I immediately looked down. I had gotten braver about eye contact. But, this was something different. I waited.

"Ledea," he seemed to be trying to choose the right word. "I've got ants in my pants, I guess, and you're just a babe in the woods."

Not knowing what to say, but noticing that Star was getting nervous because he had nothing else to say and neither did I, I started laughing and laughing loud. Hearing the *ants in your pants* after all the comments at work about t*oo big for your britches* set me off. I couldn't stop. Star started laughing, too, but then he stopped. I didn't. All his talk was just too funny. I knew he liked me, but he talked in a foreign language even though it was English.

"Ledea, what's wrong?" He asked with a hurt look on his face.

"Where are the ants?" I asked him.

"What ants?" He began looking around the picnic table and on the floor surrounding it. Apparently having forgotten about the *ants in your pants* stuff.

"The *ants in your pants*, silly," and I started laughing again.

He grabbed me by both arms, hugged me, and started laughing again. *Silly* was the most loving thing I had ever called him. And, from that point, my relationship with Star looked different and I saw him in a different way. Not scary. Not too old. I felt a connection with him. I wanted to be with Star, and he could see it.

"Hon—eey, we've got to get to know each other better. Enough of this picnic stuff. I'm takin' you to the picture show."

"I've got to get home." I immediately thought of Mel. I hadn't told her about Star. All of our dates had been afternoon picnics. I had always been home before Mel.

"Don't mean, today. Friday. Friday night. What say?" He had my hand now and was rubbing the inside of my palm with his thumb.

"I don't know." I immediately become serious. This night time stuff put a whole new look at this thing between Star and me.

"What do you mean—you don't know? The iron's hot, hon—eey."

I thought about asking him about the hot iron, but things were complicated enough as they were.

"Are you coming to the store tomorrow?" I asked him.

"Meatloaf, right?"

"Yes."

"Then, I'll be there. Will you have an answer then?" He questioned.

"Sure. I need to talk to Mel. She's my mom. I'm usually not gone at night."

His black eyebrows went up like he was surprised before he answered, "Like I said, babe in the woods."

That night while Mel and I were watching TV, I brought it up. The fact that someone had asked me to the picture show and the fact that I'd like to go. Mel was quiet for a while like she hadn't really been listening. Finally, she said something.

"Who?" It came out of her mouth while she was still watching the TV show.

"Star," was all I said.

"Star?" was all she said.

"Star." I said it again.

"Star? What kind of name is that, Ledea? Who is this person?" This time she looked at me.

"Someone I know from work. I've known him a long time. He just asked me to go with him." We both kept watching the TV not looking at each other. The Brady Bunch was on—one of our favorites--but we weren't paying attention to them either.

"I don't know, Ledea. What do you think?"

My mom had never dated anyone that I knew of since my dad—if they even ever had a date. This was a strange idea to her. I got the impression that my mom thought the two of us would just live together the rest of our lives. She had surely watched this kind of stuff on TV with the soap operas, but she had to know, I hoped, that it wasn't like that, either.

"I think he's ok, Mom. I'm 18. I'll be all right."

"Ok, Ledea." She looked at the corner of the ceiling. "Just take care."

At that, she took a deep breath like it had been a really hard day, got up without looking at me and went to the bathroom and started the shower running.

I sat there somewhat confused. Was it that easy? I wanted to be excited, but something kept me from being so. I was nervous. At night? With Star? Alone at a picture show? Out of town? Everything would be a new experience, and I didn't know if I could handle it without getting scared or just plain sick. I wasn't used to any of it.

Friday came. I didn't have to work so I spent the whole day trying on everything in my closet and even some of Mel's stuff. I washed my hair and put brush rollers in it but took them out before my hair was dry because they hurt too much. By the time Star came, my hair was shiny if not curly and I was dressed in a flowered shirt of Mel's I found in the back of her closet and a tan skirt I wore for dress-up days in high school. I put a little blush on my cheek bones although I wouldn't have needed it because my face felt hot all day just getting ready.

Star picked me up around 8:30. I was looking out the window of our house and walked out as soon as he drove up not wanting Mel to see how old he was and maybe even notice his tight pants. The picture show was an outdoor drive-in movie and wouldn't start until dark. Most of these theaters had closed down over the years, but Star explained there was one open in a town twenty miles down the road with *The Ten Commandments* showing. We drove in silence most of the way. Star looked at me once in a while and even told me I looked nice.

"Lookin' good you are, Ledea. Rome wasn't built in a day, but we'll cross that bridge when we come to it." I was confused by the talk about Rome being built, but I let it go. With Star that's what I had to do.

Star bought two tickets and found a parking spot where he hooked a box he called a speaker inside our window.

"Settled?" he asked.

"What do we do now?" I had never been to an out-door theater before.

"We wait. Unless you want popcorn. Then, we get the popcorn and come back and wait. Might as well get your feet wet, Ledea," he stated like he was in charge—which he was. "Let's go to the refreshment stand."

I climbed out of the pickup wondering about *the getting your feet wet* thing. But, Star grabbed my hand,

and I felt a little like Cinderella must have felt when she got to go the ball. Walking between other parked cars and watching all the couples sitting close, I felt in a way I had never felt before. Someone liked me. Someone besides my mom and my teacher from my school days.

The Ten Commandments was amazing. Moses parting the Red Sea, Moses getting the Ten Commandments from God, and all those people wandering in the wilderness. Although Star thought *the ten commandments* had something to do with commando or some kind of mafia-thing and was a little disappointed, my eyes were glued to the screen the whole time. Not only was it a great movie, I knew it was all true. The stories were from the Bible. It also reminded me that Mel and I had really missed a lot of Sundays going to church since my graduation from high school.

Arriving back at my house, Star came around to open the screechy pickup door that I already had opened. Closing the door behind me, he leaned against me. Within a very short period of time, I knew what the ladies at the Red Owl deli were giggling about when they talked about his pants being too tight. Our faces were inches from each other and he was out of breath for some reason.

"I need to go inside," I told him. I had had a great time at the picture show. But, I was ready to be home, get into bed and think about the movie. Star was making me uncomfortable.

"Ok, Ledea, I won't always be able to wait until the cows come home, but it's a little early, yet." He backed away from me a half step but was still breathing heavy.

Early? It was very late. I kissed him lightly on the cheek (a big thing for me as I had never kissed a man before) and turned to walk to the house when he pinned me against the truck again and gave me a kiss, if you can call it that, like none I had ever seen on a soap opera. Let's just leave it at that.

After several seconds, or minutes, I walked to the house feeling limp.

Star yelled out, "See you hon-eey. Sleep tight." I thought the entire neighborhood would hear. A few dogs started barking and I got in the house fast. Mel was asleep, thank goodness. What could I say? *The Ten Commandments*? A kiss I couldn't describe? Like I said— what could I say?

After that first night date, I started to see myself differently. I saw myself as a woman with woman capabilities. I fussed more with my hair and makeup and begged Mel to take me shopping for new clothes. I had saved money from my job and knew now what I wanted to spend it on. I looked at the JC Penney catalogs and imagined myself in some of those outfits. When I was alone I looked at the pages of underwear and wondered if women really wore that stuff to work or anywhere for that matter. Star made me look at myself differently.

Those at work saw a difference, saying—"You look different, Ledea—get a haircut? New outfit? Make-up looks nice on you." That kind of stuff. I wasn't trying to bring attention to myself. I guess I just wanted to look like Star's woman, because that's who they referred to me as. I knew he was a lot older than I was and he was different, but that didn't bother me. Star told me he loved me and being loved was like nothing I had ever expected. I felt important. I felt desired. I felt special. As Star pointed out, he was *my knight in shining armor.*

After that first picture show, we had a night-time date once a week. Sometimes, we would just drive around as Star pointed out things to me. One time, he took me to a restaurant for sea-food. I had never ordered off a menu before. Star didn't even look at the menu. Knew right away what he wanted; "crab legs," is what he said. Eating some animal's legs didn't sound good to me so I started reading all the choices. He studied me like *why you doin' that Ledea?* The waitress asked me if I needed more time, real nice about it. I saw shrimp listed and asked her for that. Mel and I had had shrimp shapes from the grocery store and I remember liking it. I didn't want Star to spend a lot of money and me not like it. They not only brought me shrimp and Star those legs of a crab, they brought fresh bread with honey in the butter, lettuce stacked high on a plate with tiny tomatoes decorating the top, and a baked potato the size of my hand. I had to share my food with Star. I had never seen so much food.

One night, he took me for a ride in the country telling me we were going to talk. He had an old quilt in the pickup when he picked me up that night. It was dark out when we left town and headed down the highway. Lightning struck here and there lighting the fields. Thunder rumbled in the distance. The air blowing in through the windows was cool and damp. I snuggled closer to Star and felt like we were on our way to never-never land. Eventually, he pulled into a driveway that led to an open field of grass or oats, I'm not sure. Star pulled the quilt out from behind the seat and jumped out; I followed getting out on his side. Even though it was dark, I could tell there were no farmhouses close by. The wind picked up and the grass blew flat. Star opened up the quilt, shook it out in the wind and slapped it down on the ground with a "Jump on it hon-ey before it gets away from us." Giggling, I jumped on the quilt and lay on my back staring up at the stormy sky. Dark clouds crisscrossed each other; they seemed to be going different directions. I felt a sprinkle or two and laughed again. I had never felt so alive.

Star lay down on his side and brought me close to him—eye to eye--and that's when he told me the story of his life. With the wind whistling over us and the thunder and lightning all around us, Star talked and talked and talked.

One of Star's first memories as a little kid was being in a large brick building with his two sisters and one brother. He was probably three or four. He remembers looking from the window to the parking lot below thinking their car looked like a toy—a miniature junker as he put it. Their mom was with them and crying a lot. Behind a humongous desk sat a mean-looking man dressed in a dark suit. After that day, Mom was gone, and the kids went to Grandma's house to live. Grandma's house was a small one-story house with broken screens sitting next to Casey's in some little town called Tin-Buck-Two. The kids slept wherever they could find a pillow and a blanket—somewhere in the house—sometimes spending all-nighters in front of the television. There was a park down the street where they played. He remembers pulling his sister off the jungle gym and breaking her arm—an accident. He also said his brother and he killed their Grandma's cat, but that it was a mean cat and tried to attack them every time they came in the house. After setting fires in their Grandma's garage, the kids were put in different foster homes. Star said they were bored that day and just wanted to see how high the flames would go.

A judge, lawyers and counselors were in and out of their lives asking them questions like, "Where would you like to live? What kind of home would you like?"
A Wisconsin couple without children of their own adopted all four of them. By the time Star was in high school, this couple had given up on the kids—getting rid of all of them except Star's sister, Lisa. After that Star had many foster homes until he turned 18. He was charged with vandalism in one town, running with some older kids when he was 12 and stealing a car, stealing cigarettes, and on and on.

I should have been scared at this point. But, I was not. I saw Star as a real person. I hadn't had an easy life either. I guess you could say that that night I melted. The shyness I once felt around him was gone.

It was very late that night when I got home. Mel was waiting at the front door. The storm outside had cleared. It kind of moved into our house because Mel was madder than I had ever seen her.

"Ledea, what are you thinking, girl?" she whispered like she had a sore throat.

"What's the matter, Mel?" I was a little worried; I had never seen Mel like this.

"What are you thinking, what are you doing? I'm askin' you. What is going on with you?"

"I was with Star…" I said real loud like because I didn't know why Mel was so mad.

"Of course, you were. Do you know what time it is?"

"No."

"It's 3 a.m. Like I said, what are you thinkin'?"

Mel had put me on the spot. I wasn't used to this from Mel. We had never fought. She had never attacked me this way. I didn't know how to answer and yet I knew I had to say something.

"Well, Star and I—we were talking."

"Talking?"

"Yes. He told me all about his life."

The look Mel gave me that night was like nothing I had seen from Mel before. It was a lost look—like she had lost something and couldn't figure out how it had happened.

Ledea and Star

Two months after that night, Star and I were married by a justice of the peace at the county court house. Mel was our witness and signed the marriage certificate. She wasn't smiling, but I can't say she was unhappy, either. More like confused. I should have understood this as Mel had only seen Star from a distance and that was sitting in his truck when he would come to pick me up. During the time Star and I were seeing each other, I tried to get him to come into our house to meet Mel. He was always in a hurry over something. It was always a relief to me—not to have him come in—thinking Mel would see something or a lot she didn't like about Star. And, what would that do to my life? It was just easier with Star not meeting Mel.

For our wedding, I had ordered a skirt and top with aqua flowers all over it out of the catalog. I wore my old sandals and curled my hair the best I could. Star had on black as usual, but his jeans were new and he had polished his boots. The justice asked him to please remove his hat before we started with all the legal words we had to say. Mel stood with her hands folded in front of her, mumbling, and checking out Star with her sideways glances.

Star explained to me that I would have to live with Mel for a while until we found a place of our own. He lived with a couple of buddies and said it wasn't a suitable place for a lady. That made me feel good—the "lady" part.

After the justice declared us to be husband and wife, Star kissed me as Mel watched, still mumbling. We all went to the local dairy sweet for ice cream. Star sat across from me on the old, wood picnic table and next to Mel—but not close. I think he did this so he wouldn't have to make eye contact with Mel. Guess they both made each other a little edgy. Mel headed home on her bike, and Star and I hopped in his pickup for our honeymoon. Star said not to pack anything—that we wouldn't be needin' a thing—we would be "foot lose and fancy free."

I had wanted Mel to say, "Congratulations, have a nice honeymoon, you look so pretty, Ledea." Any of that would have worked, but she was really caught up with all her own thoughts on my wedding day. I was so happy being Star's wife that I wasn't going to let whatever Mel thought make me feel bad.

We drove around a lot on the day of our wedding with Star doing most of the talking. Star said that I was just a babe in the woods and something else about a one-eyed snake. He went on and on. Finally, he almost shouted, "I'm grasping at straws, here, hon-ey, help me out!"

I felt that he was mad at me for some reason. I almost started to cry. Then, I took a deep breath and said to myself, *Ledea, you're married. This is your husband. You should be able to talk to him about anything.* And so, I blurted out, "Star, what's the matter?"

"Matter?" He shook his head from side to side.

"Why are you so mad?"

"Well, hon-ey, you're not the sharpest tool in the shed."

I could tell he was mad at me and I had no idea why.

"Star, what is this stuff about a shed, the woods, a snake?" Now, my voice was rising. "I don't understand you. Just tell me what you mean."

Star turned and looked out the window and said, "Never mind."

After a few minutes and me thinking it was too quiet, I turned on the radio to his favorite country station and before long Star was singing real loud-like along with somebody named Travis. I was glad he was happy again. We drove until dark, stopped at a Henry's for burgers and fries and then looked for a place to stay. Star seemed to know where to go although he said we had no reservations. We came to a Motel 6. Star told me to stay in the car—he'd be right back. He was.

"Git down in the seat hon-ey. I paid for just one of us."

"Star?"

"Git down!"

Star had never been that bossy with me before. I didn't grow up with a dad. Was this the way it was to be?

Although a little embarrassed, I made it through our first night together. I had no daydreams about what this would be like. Mel had never talked to me about it. I didn't have girlfriends who talked about these kinds of things. And the soap operas that Maria and I had watched didn't even get into this stuff probably because it was the kind of thing you weren't supposed to see on TV. Star used the babe in the woods and one-eyed snake words a lot. It was both good and bad. I guessed I could get used to it.

God

Star and I started our lives together with me living with Mel and Star living with his buddies in a place I never had a chance to visit. Star said that was best. He came over some nights late when Mel was already asleep—saying he didn't want no trouble with a mother-in-law.

I bring the God part in now because after I got married I started thinking about a lot of things. About being a woman. About being married. About Mel and me and about our past. Somehow, we had gotten away from going to church. All that stuff I wrote about Star and me—no mention of God. Right? Well, it's what happened. I got so tied up with thinking about Star that I stopped thinking about God. And, I have to admit that it started even before Star came along. After my high school graduation, Mel and I started watching movies a lot on Saturday nights and sleeping in on Sunday mornings. We got in a real habit of this. Pastor Simmons called us once or twice. We made excuses, but we really had no good ones. We might have gone on and on like this except that something big happened. God didn't cause it, but he did get my attention.

It was on television and in the newspaper. The cops came to the Red Owl to get me. They walked right up to the deli. I thought they were there to order. When one of them said, "Ledea Jenkins, please," I knew it wasn't food they were after.

"Yes, I'm Ledea." I was already taking off my Red Owl apron.

"There's been an accident," the biggest one said. The first person I thought of was Star. He was a little reckless. This part of him scared me and attracted me to him at the same time.

"Are you the daughter of Mel Jenkins?" the little guy asked.

"Mel? Where is she? What happened," I blurted.

"There's been an accident," one of them said.

"She doesn't drive. We don't own a car." I was trying to understand.

"Someone hit her while she was riding her bike."

"Oh, dear God," I said soft-like—not like someone might do when they are swearing. We didn't talk like that in our house.

"She's in the hospital," the little guy said watching me real careful. Without saying anything else, I ran out of the store with the cops following me saying, "Slow down, we'll take you there." Sitting quietly in the back of the cop car, my hands and legs were shaking up and down and sideways. I was afraid to ask how she was.

The driver made eye contact through the rear view mirror.

"So, you're Mel's daughter?" he questioned.

I nodded but didn't say anything. I was too worried about Mel. Besides, he had already asked me that.

"Weren't you in an accident a year or so ago? Out on the county gravel road with a bunch of others?" He was looking at me like he was trying to find something wrong with me.

I nodded again. The leg-shaking was getting worse. Pressing on my knees with my hands, I tried to stop my body from doing dumb things on its own.

"The Jackson boy, Rick, he was killed in that accident," the other officer said.

"My mother, how is she?" I could not stand the suspense.

"Oh, sure," the driver said. "Your mother was knocked unconscious. They're not sure of her injuries, yet. We just thought you should be there. Any other family?"

I thought of my grandparents—pretty much stuck in their own house because of poor health. Mel and I hadn't seen them in a while.

"No. Just me…. And Star," I suddenly thought of him.

"Star?"

"My husband. Can you let him know, too?" They both looked at each other like—*can you believe she's married*?

"Sure. Does this Star have a last name?" the guy on the passenger side asked turning to look straight at me when he asked.

"Johnson. Star Johnson."

One of the officers coughed. The other one did a funny noise through his nose.

"Star Johnson? You mean, Stanley Johnson?"

"Star," I repeated. Why couldn't they get it right the first time?

"Guess that one got by us—Stanley getting married," the cop on the passenger side said. I wondered why he was laughing. My mom had been in an accident, and we were on our way to the hospital.

"It's Star. My husband's name is Star Johnson. And my name is Ledea Johnson, not Ledea Jenkins." I was getting mad. My mother was hurt, and they were talking about some Stanley Johnson.

Mel was still in the emergency room when we got to the hospital. She had scratches and big red welts on her face and arms. They had already given stitches to some of her cuts. She was pretty out of it, but she did smile sort of when she saw me. While riding her bike home from work, she had swerved, hit the curb and bounced back into traffic. A car hit her or she hit the car. I'm not sure about that. Anyway, the doctors, nurses, and cops said she was lucky it wasn't worse. After a short visit, the cops offered me a ride home. I said no, stayed with Mel until she fell asleep and then walked home. I wanted to be alone and I really didn't care for the way they had treated me.

Star didn't come that night. I didn't always know when he would be coming. We had no phone. I usually saw him at the Red Owl or he would come by after supper to Mel's. I hadn't seen him either place. With Mel still in the hospital, I felt very alone. I watched TV hoping he would come. I really needed to tell someone. I went to bed late and left the door unlocked. Sometimes, Star would come during the night, and we would sleep together before he got up the next day to go to work.

Around midnight I got up—not being able to sleep. I pulled a blanket around me and looked out the front window hoping to see Star's pickup. The street was empty. Sitting on Mel's lumpy couch, I stared at the wall and soon dozed off. It was then that I had the dream about Maria. I saw her everywhere. We were walking together—just like old times. She was beside me at work although I could tell no one else could see her. And, she was by my mother in the hospital. In my dream, the words that were coming out of my mouth to Maria were all gibberish—stuff I didn't understand. But, I did understand Maria's words to me. Whenever she moved her lips, she said, "God loves you, Ledea." Over and over and over. These words made me not only miss Maria; they made me miss God. There was an empty feeling inside me—a place where God used to be.

I woke up early the next day hungry. After grabbing a bowl of cold cereal and milk, I sat in front of our old TV and turned on the morning news. The weather was cloudy with chance of rain. The local news didn't get my attention until the newscaster said,

"Middle-aged woman hit by car while riding bike on her way home from work." I sat on the edge of the couch as I watched some traffic on the screen and then Mel's wrecked bike. By-standers were shaking their heads and pointing. I grabbed my coat, left my cereal and was out the door.

Mel was up and sipping something through a straw when I arrived. I could tell she hurt all over. She was more swollen than the day before. She was glad to see me. We talked about stuff, like, what can you eat, when will you be able to come home, where does it hurt? Mel wasn't too excited about talking, but she did her best.

I had trouble concentrating at work that day. Would Mel be ok? Where was Star? Back and forth. It was a meat-loaf special day, and we ran out early. So besides thinking about Mel and Star, I had to keep explaining to people about the meat loaf.

Around 2 p.m., Star came in faster than usual— walking straight to the deli.

"Star, I've been wanting to talk to you." I didn't know whether to be mad or relieved that, at least, he was ok.

Everyone at work had asked about my mom. They had either been at the Red Owl when the cops came to get me or they had heard it on the news or from each other. How would I tell Star in front of everyone— especially when I was supposed to be serving customers? It ended up that I didn't have to worry about that. Star already knew.

"And, I'm wanting to talk to you." His eyes were sparkly for some reason—the way he gets when he wants to tease or have fun.

"No. Star, this is serious. It's my mom…."

"I know, Ledea. She's hurt bad, right? Let the chips fall where they may, Ledea; we got to do the right thing with this."

I was confused as usual when Star got on a roll with the words he used.

"I'm not sure what you mean, Star, but Mel is going to be ok. She'll come home in a couple of days."

"What?"

"She's going to be ok."

"Oh….guess I heard differently." If you can act surprised and disappointed at the same time, that was Star.

"No. She's going to be ok," I repeated.

"Give me the meat loaf special, Ledea. I'll be over after work."

"Star, the meat loaf is gone."

"Where'd it go?"

"People ate it up already. There is none." I said kind of loud-like. Star was starting to get to me.

"Ok. Ok. Let's go with the chicken, then. Always a favorite of mine. Right Ledea?"

So I dished up his chicken, dark meat, lots of gravy and Star left. Like I said earlier, I was upset with Star. One of my co-workers always said of her husband, *Can't live with him; can't live without him*. Maybe there were just some things we were not supposed to understand about each other — the opposite sex, that is.

Star did come that night — early — and asked what we were having for supper. I wasn't used to having Star at our house for supper. I dug around in the freezer and found some fish sticks and tater tots and stuck them in the oven. I sat on the couch next to Star while they heated up wanting to talk to him about Mel and my dream about Maria and God. He was complaining about no remote control, getting up and down to change channels. I finally turned it off — real brave of me — his eyebrows went up when I did it.

"Star. We need to talk. My mom is going to be ok. But, I want to talk to you about something else. It's kind of important."

"Does your mom own the house?" Just like that it came out. Like I said, when Star got on a roll with his words, I was often confused. But, this was like he hadn't even heard the stuff I had said.

"What?" I asked.

"Does your mom own this house?" He was looking at me like I was the stupid one for not getting his question.

"I… I don't know. We've always lived here. Why are you asking me?"

"Well, silly, it's just something we need to know. This was just an accident, but your mom is not going to live forever, you know. No one does." He laughed as if this were a joke of some kind.

"How old is she?" Star grinned like we were on a quiz show or something.

His questions were starting to bother me. I wanted to talk to Star about God, and he was asking me questions about who owned our house and how old was Mel. I didn't know whether to cry or be angry.

"Or, don't you know that either?" With this question, he stopped grinning and almost looked mad.

I stared at him and said not a thing. Star was staring back with a look I had never seen. The way someone looks at you when you know they don't like you. No, I didn't know who owned our house, but I did know how old Mel was. We had just celebrated her 38th birthday before Star and I married. Did he think 38 was old? My grandparents were *old*; Mel was not. I was starting to think that maybe Star was not so smart.

I walked out to the kitchen, took the fish sticks and tater tots from the oven, got some plastic plates down from the cupboard and sat down to eat. Star came out and sat across from me. I folded my hands in prayer. He looked at me funny-like. This was my chance to talk about God.

"Come Lord Jesus," I stared at Star real serious, and, then bowed my head for the "be our guest. Let these gifts to us be blessed. Amen."

Star stared at me like I was funny in the head. I didn't know how else to bring up God and we were getting ready to eat. It just came out. The prayer, that is. Mel and I used to say it when I was little. I don't know why we stopped.

"What was that all about?" Star questioned me grabbing fish sticks and tater totts—more than his share.

"Mel and I used to pray before we ate," I explained.

"Well, hon-ee, Mel's not here, so skip the religious stuff."

I touched his hand that was headed for the fish sticks on his plate to get his attention.

"Star, do you believe in God?"

"God? God, who?"

"Do you believe in God?" I needed to know.

"I'm agnostic, Ledea. Let's drop it."

"Egg what?" Star was using those big, different words on me, again.

"Egg what?" He said what I said. "Doesn't that beat all. If you want to know why I'm *egg*-nostic, I'll tell you. God ain't done nothin' for me, Ledea. I'm a self-made man. Don't need him."

"Everyone needs God, Star. He created us. We belong to him." I don't know where the words were coming from but they kept coming. "We're all a part of his family. We're all connected in some way, and someday we will all have eternal life with him if only we believe."

Star looked puzzled, started eating fish sticks and then said, "Ledea, that's the most you ever said at one time. Next, you'll be wantin' me to go to church. Just so you understand—I ain't goin'. Now you. If that's for you, then you go. Probably make us both look good." And then he smiled like he was finally pleased with me.

And, I started to think that that is exactly what I needed to do. Go to church.

Pastor Simmons

Each of us is only one. Although only one, we have no right to minimize what God can do when we allow him to work through us. If we are willing and sincerely ask, "What will you have me do?" the possibilities may be endless. He opens our eyes, stirs our wills, and shows us open doors. Now you may be thinking, "I have no special gifts or talents." ... or "You know, God, I'm just a regular guy...I'm not even very capable or competent in a lot of what I have to do in a normal day." But, if you open your heart to him, he will make your efforts effective in new and wonderful ways.

Pastor Simmons had me spellbound. Mel sat beside me in church—spellbound, too. After the Lord's Prayer and Pastor Simmons saying "Go in peace and serve the Lord," Mel and I just sat. I don't know if we were thinking about the sermon or if it just felt good to be back in church—maybe both. While we were sitting, people came up to us saying things like, "Where have you been? Nice to have you back? Heard you were in an accident, Mel. You ok, now?"

As we left that day, Pastor Simmons asked if he could visit us. *Would this afternoon work,* he asked. Mel and I nodded yes but wondered why as we left the church. Had we done something wrong? Had we not given enough money? Were we no longer welcomed?

Star was at work, or at least that is what he said, so it was just me and Mel for Sunday dinner—Banquet Fried Chicken with mashed potatoes and corn. We got out the chocolate instant pudding for dessert. It whips up really fast. We picked up the house, took out the trash, and shook the rugs still wondering why Pastor Simmons wanted to visit. He had seen us in church and even came to the hospital when Mel was there. We were curious and a little scared. Mel got out the ice tea mix and some tall, plastic glasses and then we sat and waited mostly staring at the clock.

It was a nice day. The windows were open and a few flies had gotten in through the holes in the screens. I got up to get a flyswatter when I heard a knock on the door. Mel and I both jumped a little. Except for Star once in a while, Maria was the only person who had visited us. And, of course, she was gone.

While I was swatting flies, Mel let Pastor Simmons in and offered him a seat on our couch. I noticed for the first time how far down the couch went when Pastor Simmons sat, and he was not a big man. Mel sat in the only other chair. They both looked at me, so I put the swatter down and sat on the other side of the couch hands between my knees.

"It was good to see you both in church this morning," he said with a nice smile on his face. We smiled back, waiting.

"I apologize for not getting here sooner. It's been on my list of things to do—just haven't gotten it done."

He looked at us. We smiled. Waiting and worrying just a little.

"Mel, you're feeling better, I hope. Are you back to work?" He pulled himself forward on the couch and looked right at Mel.

"Yea. I'm back and feeling pretty good. Ledea's been a good help around the house." At this, Pastor Simmons looked relieved. Maybe, it was because somebody else finally talked besides himself.

"That's good, but I hear you're married Ledea. It's good you've been able to help your mom."

"Oh, that's not a problem. I live here. Star and I haven't found a place, yet. So, this works out for now."

"I see. Star? Do I know your husband? I'd like to meet him."

"Star Johnson. I met him while he was ordering chicken. At the deli. At the Red Owl." I blushed at this—remembering—which made Pastor Simmons smile.

"Star Johnson," he repeated. "Would that be Stanley?" He had his eyebrows up. I didn't know why people kept thinking Star was Stanley. I thought Star signed his name *Star* on our marriage certificate. You had to do it just right they had said at the court house—your exact name—the name given at birth.

"Just Star," I answered. His eyebrows went down and he nodded his head as if he understood. While Pastor Simmons and Mel visited about the weather and a little about our neighborhood, I looked him over. He looked different sitting in our house. I noticed that his shoes were a little worn looking, his trousers a little thin at the knees. He had these light blue bags under his eyes and he looked tired. I got up to get the iced tea. When I was in the kitchen I heard Pastor Simmons ask Mel about me getting married to Star—things like where we were married, where did Star work—that kind of thing. When I brought the iced tea back, he stopped and changed the subject.

"Ledea, I remember you as a little girl coming up to children's sermon," he said taking the iced tea from me. I wiped my cold, wet hand on my pants and waited to see what else he had to say.

"You were always so eager. One of the first to come up. You listened ever so carefully." This got me going. I finally had something to talk about.

"I used to memorize some of the passages from the Bible you read at church. And, some of the hymns, too. I had a lot of favorites. They always made me feel special. It was good to know that God loved me so much."

"God loved you so much," he smiled the kind of smile that lights up one's whole face, "and he still does."

I don't know why, but Pastor Simmons saying it this way and looking the way he did made me cry. I sat on my side of the couch with my head in my hands and cried these great big tears not knowing where they came from or why. He leaned toward me and gently rubbed my back between the shoulders with the palm of his hand.

"God loved you so much as a child, Ledea," he repeated, "and he still does as an adult. Never forget that."

For some reason a bunch of funny memories came back to me. Not the ha-ha kind. Things I never thought about much before as a child or an adult came running through my mind like a fast forward on a video. Pictures in my mind of little girls in fancy dresses at Easter; little girls with over-night bags going to each other's slumber parties; little girls going to dance classes, piano lessons, gymnastics and swimming lessons. An outsider, that's what I was. Little girls with fathers—holding their hands, sharing a hymnal, rubbing their backs during church. For the first time in my life, I felt I had missed out by not having a loving father. So, I cried and cried. How could I explain this to Mel or Pastor Simmons?

Pastor Simmons handed me his white handkerchief and I wiped my face dry. I don't know why but I felt better. When I looked at Mel, she looked puzzled with a *what-has-gotten-into-you?* look on her face. I handed the wet hanky back to Pastor Simmons with a thank you.

"I'm glad you were in church today and I hope you can keep coming. Our church does not always do a very good job of letting people know that we miss them when they stop coming, but we need to." He gave my back a final pat, stood, and handed me his empty iced tea glass.

"Thanks for coming," I said. Mel was still puzzled. She said nothing.

"Before I go, I just want to make sure you remember all the things the church has to offer. Oh, and we need help once in a while, too." He added with a chuckle. "For example, our Sunday School needs helpers. You'd be good with little children, Ledea. What do you think?"

"What do you want me to do?" I wondered.

"Well, just show up. We'll tell you where to go. You could help with crafts, getting the kids organized, that kind of thing. An extra pair of hands is always appreciated." I smiled. I could do that.

"And, Mel. Someone told me that you have this beautiful voice. Have you ever considered joining the choir? We practice once a week on Wednesday nights." Mel blushed at this. "Don't need to decide tonight. Just give it some thought."

As he walked toward the door, Pastor Simmons seemed to be checking out all his pockets. He pulled out a small radio that was about half the size of the palm of his hand. Attached to it was a cord with an ear plug.

"Ledea, this is for you. I know you walk to and from work every day. I recommend KJCY. It's already set on 95.5. It's Christian radio —lots of good music, a little news and spiritual talks. I think you'll like it."

"Wow. Thanks." He placed it in my hands. I couldn't stop smiling. I had never had a radio of my own. We had an old one in our kitchen where we listened to the weather once in a while when Mel and I ate breakfast. This one could go with me everywhere.

"If you need new batteries, let me know. I can help you out with that one—especially the first time—I can show you how to change them."

"Thank you, Pastor Simmons." And, I gave him a hug. Mel shook his hand just like she does when we're leaving church. Guess she was comfortable with that.

When the door slammed shut, Mel and I looked at each other with a bit of wonder in our eyes.

"I think I'll try choir," Mel said.

"I think you should." We both nodded our heads agreeing it was a great idea.

"And, I can help with Sunday School. Right?"

"Yes, you can." Mel and I smiled at each other. It felt like it was old times when we never missed a Sunday and always felt so good about going and being a part of the church. I was really glad Pastor Simmons decided to visit.

On the following Wednesday, Mel became a part of the choir. It made me really proud to see her singing with the rest of them. She looked different—so much joy on her face. I was happy for her. I helped with Sunday School for several weeks. The children were gentle, sweet, and very busy. However, Star soon made a decision that would make it impossible for me to help with Sunday School or go to Pastor Simmons' church for a long time.

Star

Whatever you might consider normal in our lives—that's what it was for several weeks after Pastor Simmons visited. Except, Mel and I were going back to church. We were both happier because of it. One

Sunday as I was leaving, Pastor Simmons placed a Bible in my hands. "It's for you Ledea," was all he said.

When Star saw it sitting on my dresser, he asked, "What's this? 'Gettin' big ideas, are ya?'"

"No. It's a Bible, Star. Pastor Simmons...." But before I could finish he interrupted me.

"You're nutty as a fruitcake sometimes Ledea," he said to himself while shaking his head back and forth. "Sometimes I wonder what I got myself into."

"What do you mean, Star? It's just a Bi...."

"Nutty as a fruitcake," he repeated. "Sit down. We need to talk. This is comin' at you straight from the horse's mouth. You need to pull yourself together because we're pulling up stakes. Like today."

"What?" Star was making less sense than usual.

"What are you saying to me, Star?" I asked again.

"It's time you and me had a place of our own. Nothing against Mel. Don't get me wrong. She's a good woman. We're married, Ledea, dang it. We need to have a place of our own."

"But where? We have no place."

"Well, things have changed. The guys that I've been livin' with. They're gone. Got up and left. Just like that. Left the whole place to me. Lock, stock, and barrel."

"Lock, stock, and what?" I asked.

"Never mind. Just trust me. You're going to get your feet wet."

"Why would I do that?" I mumbled. Star was on the verge of making me sick. He was talking fast and making no sense. His eyes were darting about and he acted like he had jumping beans inside him. I wanted to run away from him until he settled down.

He ignored my question.

"We're goin' to be burnin' the candle at both ends. Best we get started." Star was talking a so fast I had to listen closely. He was my husband; I would try to understand what he wanted.

"Star, what do you want me to do?"

"Now, you're talkin'. I'm not goin' to beat around the bush. Pack your things. Everything. Mel got extra stuff? Take that, too. You know—kitchen stuff. Got that?"

"Star, where are we going?"

"Our place, baby." With this, he smiled. And, so, I packed.

Within a half hour I had packed an old suitcase with all my clothing, some things from the bathroom, the Bible and small radio Pastor Simmons had given me. Star brought in a cardboard box and started taking a few things from the kitchen—a frying pan, a cake pan, some salt, some flour and a couple of boxes of hamburger helper. Then, he went into the bathroom and took some towels. On his way out, he stopped in my bedroom and took the sheets, blankets, and pillows from my bed and stuffed them in the box with the kitchen things. I was hoping Mel wouldn't miss any of it.

While Star was running things out to his pickup, I found an old envelope and wrote a note to Mel.

Everything had happened so fast, I really didn't know what to write.

Dear Mel, Star has found a place for us to live. I took some of my stuff and some of your stuff. I hope that is ok. I'll call you when we get there. Love you, Ledea

I hopped in the passenger side of Star's pickup and we roared off-- me wondering why the big hurry. Star turned on the radio to some country station—LOUD— and sang as if I were not even there. Somebody named Jerry Reed was singing, "When you're hot, you're hot; when you're not, you're not.." and more stuff about rollin' dice and good luck. I was beginning to wonder if I really knew this person and here I was married to him and running off to never-never-land.

Miles and miles went by. I had never been so far away from home. We kept on with the country music station. Star was quiet during some of the songs and loud during others. Somebody named Steve sang "All Roads Lead to You." Steve, the singer, said he thought he could forget, but he couldn't (talking about his girl, I guess) and then said something that really got my attention: *if I could just turnoff my mind, I'd be all right.* So, you see, that is what I tried to do: turn off my mind. Instead of trying to figure everything out, I stared at the telephone poles passing and the fields letting my brain go blank. A couple of hours, a lot of telephone poles and fields passed before Star turned on a one-lane gravel road with a lot of bumps and holes. After a minute or two, he slowed down and turned again to a dirt-like narrow road that had trees on both sides. Cool air rushed in the windows as the sun was blocked out. It felt good. I almost smiled. Maybe, this would be ok. Star took a sharp turn and stomped on the brake with his big boot. Star's driving made me bump his shoulder and then hit my head on the dash. When I sat up, there, in front of me was a small cottage on a little hill.

Star turned off the radio, turned off the pickup and looked at me for the first time during our ride. "Home sweet, home, hon—ey!" He laughed out loud. And, I laughed. If Star was this happy, it must be good.

"Let me show you around. Then, we'll start unpackin'. Shake a leg."

Just for fun as I stepped out of the pickup, I shook my leg. Star didn't always make sense, but I guess I could at least have some fun with it.

There was a little stone path that led up to the cottage. The cottage was covered with brown shingles— some of them loose. There were two windows facing us and a door with peeling paint. Using his shoulder, Star pushed the door open, scooped me up like I was a kid and carried me in. I noticed the smell first. It came at me fast. I had never smelled anything like it. Sweet, smoky, old, mildewy—all rolled into one. A little bit like Maria's house used to smell but other smells, too.

"We'll need to air it out," Star stated as he put me down and went around opening windows.

It was one big room with a divider half way up the middle. On the other side of the divider was an old bed, a small tilted bed stand and a dresser with a cracked mirror. The other room had a sink, small refrigerator, gas stove, and wooden table with some chairs pushed under it. At the other end, there was an old plaid couch and a TV sitting on a dusty table. A rag rug lay in front of the couch. It was dirty like someone with muddy shoes had walked on it.

"Wow," I said. I didn't mean wow like you think of it. It just came out. It was the kind of *wow* that meant—I can't believe this, is this where we're going to live, who used to live here, how far are we from anything, and what is that smell—wow.

"Yea, you're goin' love it." Star was still on a roll. "Once it's cleaned up, it'll be perfect. Our first home." Star was at a backdoor I hadn't noticed before shoving it open. I followed him out and up another path of a smaller hill. Grass grew on both sides with a few wild flowers here and there. We walked about fifty steps before Star stopped in front of me—me bumping into his back. He took me by the hand and brought me to his side.

"Look, hon—ey. Isn't that pretty?"

And there in front of us was this lake. A *lake!*

"Star." I could say nothing else.

We both stood in the late afternoon sun looking at this blue lake and holding hands. Grass grew where it was shallow and the waves lapped lightly at the shore line. There was some sand, some weeds. Birds were singing and crickets chirping. A frog croaked. As I looked across the lake, it seemed to go on forever. In the distance there were lots of trees and spots of color here and there—perhaps houses.

"Star, is this ours?" I felt almost scared.

"The cottage is ours—for now. The lake belongs to lots of people. Some of them rich—on the other side over there. Do you like it?"

"It's so pretty."

"Yea, I guess you could say we hit the jackpot, Ledea. It's ours for now. Now, let's make hay while the sun shines."

With that Star headed back to the truck with me following. We hauled everything from the truck into the house. Next, Star went to a cupboard below the sink and got out some dish soap, rags and a plastic bucket. He filled it with water, squirted some soap in and handed me one of the rags.

"You get started, hon—ey. I got some things to check out."

I didn't know where to start. The sink was gross. I could not see out the windows. Every flat surface in the house was dusty and sticky. I noticed junk in the corners of the house—like old clothes and cans and empty boxes of food—and wondered who could have lived here. Where would I start? Hearing Star's pickup throw gravel, I sat on the lumpy couch and wondered if Mel was thinking about me. Had she read the note? Was she worried? I started to miss her, my mom. We had always been together. And then I thought about Pastor Simmons. I had just started going back to church. Would I ever see him, again? Feeling sorry for myself would get me no where. What is it Ms. Stenzel used to say? *Concentrate on your strengths.* More stuff started coming back—like one of my favorite Bible verses—*The secret is Christ is in me.* Stop feeling sorry for yourself, Ledea, I told myself.

Digging out the little transistor Pastor Simmons had given me, I turned it on. Listening to KJCY—Know Jesus Cares for You—gave me the energy I needed to dig in. After a couple hours and several buckets of soapy water, our house was not perfect but cleaner than it had been. I even took the sheets Star had stripped from my bed, washed them in the sink and hung them on a clothes line I found by the side of the house. After hanging them, I took the path back to the lake. The sun sparkled off the water and hurt my eyes. Taking off my shoes, I waded in and felt the sand between my toes and the cool water on my ankles. I saw a bird standing perfectly straight on some tall grass—with red on its black wings singing chirp-chirp. I felt good. I rinsed off my face and arms in the clear lake water and then heard the sound of Star's pickup. I ran back to the little house.

As I entered the house, I could still smell that funny smell, but the house kind of sparkled it was so clean. Star even noticed. He picked me up, swung me around in a circle and kissed me on the neck. A sucky kind of kiss—one of his favorites.

"Got food. Our favorite. Chicken, potatoes, and gravy."

My heart did a little hurtful jump when I heard this—as in, *Star you were in town? At the Red Owl?* But, I didn't say anything. I *was* hungry. We stuffed ourselves with chicken, mashed potatoes and gravy at our table in our house. As Star was finishing, I asked him what had been on my mind.

"What about my job?" he was cleaning off the bones with his teeth as he always did.

"Oh, you did good, hon—ey. You made a silk purse out of this sow's ear." And he grinned like some little kid.

"Star? Purse? Ear?" I could pretend I understood Star on some of his stuff. But, there were no silk purses or pigs around here.

"Don't worry. You did a good job. Spick and Span."

"Star. My job. I'm supposed to work tomorrow. Can you take me?"

He rubbed his forehead and looked out one of our now see-through windows.

"Ledea, we've got to throw caution to the wind and turn over a new leaf. I've got some skeletons in my closet and well, things have got to change."

"My job. Can you take me tomorrow? That's all I want to know." I asked again.

"Ledea, you're not getin' it." At this, he took my hands in his. "You'll have to find a new job. I told them at the Red Owl that you was quittin'."

"What? I like my job, Star."

"Well, it's a done thing. So best you put it behind you."

"What am I supposed to do?" I looked around me. This house was ours—Star's and mine, but I could not imagine staying here day after day and never having anywhere to go. And, how would we live? Star had already started to use part of my Red Owl check when I lived with Mel.

"Star. We need money. We have no food in this house."

"Don't think I don't know that. We're not up a creek without a paddle yet, Ledea. I got an idea if you just listen." I think he was kind of getting mad—me asking so many questions—like maybe this idea of his was not the greatest idea in the world.

"When I was in town, I took this newspaper—the ad section. Here, I ripped it out. Let me show you." At this he pulled out a wrinkled little piece of paper from his shirt pocket and handed it to me. It read: "Wanted: housekeeper. Three days a week. Will train. Call Katherine Wilson at 555-......" It was highlighted in yellow.

"Star, you want me to do this? I don't know her."

"Don't matter. Don't need to know someone to apply for a job. Did you know any of those people at the Red Owl, Ledea, when you applied?" I shook my head no.

"Good. Then, let's not get cold feet over this. What did it say? Read it to me, Ledea."

I wondered why he just didn't read it himself. He with his big ideas.

I read it out loud this time and then said, "Star, we have no phone."

"Not a problem. I know where Katherine Wilson lives. Come with me."

Star didn't head for the pickup. He headed out the back door, up the path to the lake; but instead of walking directly to the lake, he took another path that led around the lake. I hadn't noticed it before as it was covered with more grass than the lake path. I followed him—a few steps behind—neither of us saying anything. It was early evening by this time; the sun was setting. My stomach was full and it felt good to use my legs. Farther down the road, there were more trees and shade covered the path. I started to see those far-a-way specks of color up close. The first houses were small and cute looking with flowers surrounding them. As we walked farther, the houses got bigger. Some were like mansions. Others reminded me of castles. I had never seen anything like them. There were big porches wrapped around them, stone paths, and large flower gardens with hanging plants and colorful, trimmed bushes.

"Star, what is this place?" I broke the silence.

"It's called The Lake Village. Rich people live on this side of the lake. There's a small grocery, food stands, bait shops, lots of docks and boats and skiers—all that stuff. Some people live here just in the summer—some live here year around. Anyway, Katherine Wilson? She lives right there. In a nutshell." Star stopped, and, again, I ran into his backside as I was trying to take everything in.

It didn't look like a nutshell to me. It was one of the most beautiful houses I had ever seen. A wide, cement walkway lead to a three-story white house with a porch that wrapped around the three sides facing the lake. Four hanging swings hung from the porch ceiling. Pots of colorful flowers were placed on the steps and around the porch. Hanging plants swung lightly with the lake breeze. The windows were shiny and reflected the lake.

Star pushed me forward.

"Star. Stop. What are you doing?" I pushed his hands away that kept pushing at my backside.

"The ad. Remember, Ledea, the ad. Put your best foot forward." Without thinking, I looked down at my foot, although I *knew* this time what Star wanted me to do.

"Star, I won't know what to say. Look at me."

"Are you worried about what to say or how you look?" Star was starting to get a little mad at me. His hands were on his hips. The problem with Star was that he wanted things to happen and happen right now. Even when he ordered his chicken, he would start to stand on one foot and then another, start looking around as if he had someplace to go real quick. I now understood "ants in your pants," and Star had a serious case of them.

"Both," I answered.

Star looked at me from head to toe and I knew what he was seeing. I pushed my glasses up on my nose, pulled my fingers through my hair and stomped my feet so some of the dirt and dust would be off my worn tennis shoes. Star smiled, took two of his fingers, licked them and then rubbed the side of my mouth.

"Just a little gravy, Ledea. You're lookin' good. No problem." Again, he gave my backside a shove toward the house.

"Star. Stop. What do I say?"

"Say—*I saw your ad. When do you want me to start*?"

I was again thinking that Star was not too smart. I had learned in school and through my job site a little about what to say and how to act when a person is looking for a job. He gave me another shove. I have to admit I had mixed feelings at this point. I was a little mad, a little scared, and also a little excited that I could work in a place that looked like this. A part of me also wanted to believe that Star really thought I could get this job. That, he believed in me. And, so I walked those fifty steps (counting all of them) up the walk and knocked on Katherine Wilson's door.

Katherine Wilson

Katherine Wilson was probably the most beautiful person I had ever seen. She answered the door on my second knock saying "Hi!" with a huge smile that showed these perfectly straight, white teeth. She had on a t-shirt with baggy shorts and flip-flops on her feet. Her hair was long, orange-red, and hung in curly-cues. She had this look on her face, like *what can I do for you?*

"Ummm—Could I speak to Katherine Wilson, please?" This couldn't be Katherine, I thought, maybe her daughter. I put my head down and spotted her perfect, clean feet with each toenail polished in a shiny orange color that almost matched her hair.

"I'm Katherine." She waited for me to raise my head, looked at me carefully, and then blurted out, "Did you see my ad in the paper?"

"Yes. That's why I'm here." Taking a deep breath, I felt better already.

"Forgive my bad manners. Please come in." And she spread her arm out towards her house to welcome me. I wanted to look back to see if Star was still at the end of Katherine's walkway, but I couldn't pull my eyes away from the house. Kicking off my shoes, my feet sank in deep carpet. Couches, some with flowers and some in matching plain colors, were all about the room with shiny lamps beside them.

When I stopped looking around, I noticed she was staring at me. Remembering that I had not said my name, I stuck my hand out and said, "I'm Ledea Jenkins, I mean Ledea Johnson and I'm looking for a job."

She smiled. "Lydia, that's a pretty name."

"Thanks. My dad named me. He gave a different spelling to it. L-e-d-e-a, but it's pronounced the same as the other Lydia." Katherine just smiled and nodded.

"Please, let's go to the kitchen. Do you drink coffee?" She asked.

"Well, I guess I could." If it meant getting the job—I could drink coffee.

"How about lemonade or orange juice?" Katherine offered.

"Lemonade." I looked at her with her clear skin and then remembered my manners. "Thank you."

"So, you saw my ad. Sit down please. I'll get the lemonade and then we can talk."

Katherine treated me like I was the perfect person to work for her. She explained that she was very particular and that's why she needed some help. She was active in a lot of groups, had two younger children and had very little time for the house. Could I start work tomorrow? How many days a week could I work? She would show me how everything was to be done. There would be a list to follow while she was gone, but we would also work together. My head was swimming. I hadn't touched my lemonade I was so busy listening to her and taking it all in.

"Yes," I finally said when she stopped talking.

"Great!" and as she smiled at me, two kids ran into the room chasing each other. "Hold your horses. Kendra, Kyle—I want you to meet someone." They stopped surprised that someone was in their house and quieted down.

"I'd like you to meet Ledea. Ledea, this is my daughter, Kendra, and my son, Kyle. Kendra's in pre-school and Kyle is in second grade."

"Hi," they both said at the same time while checking me out from head to toe.

"Hi," I answered as they continued to stare at me—including my bare feet. Somehow I felt small and skinny around them even though they were only children.

"You both need to get your jammies on; it's getting late." The kids ran off and Katherine turned back to me.

"What time should I come tomorrow?" I asked. With that question, she seemed to think about something.

"Ledea, do you drive? Do you have a car?"

"Ummm, no. But I walked today. I live on the other side of the lake."

She frowned at me—like *are you sure?*

"You can't see it from here, but it's down the path and over a little hill. It's all by itself—just a little house. We just moved in today."

"I think I know what you mean. It's a small, brown-shingled house. Stood empty for some time, I believe. You're living there?" I nodded, looked around this house with all its beautiful things not knowing for sure what she thought of me and where I lived.
"It's a long walk, Ledea. Do I need to pick you up?"

"No. Star can bring me or I'll walk. I did today and it didn't seem long at all."

"Star?" she looked puzzled.

"Yes, Star. He's my husband." I didn't say *husband* very often and it kind of made me blush.

Katherine only smiled and took a deep breath. I couldn't tell if she was relieved that I didn't live by myself in that little brown house or if she was relieved that she finally had someone to clean her house.

"OK. Then, it's settled. I'll see you tomorrow at 9. Then, we can go over everything."

I realized I hadn't touched my lemonade and gulped it down while Katherine watched me. I really was thirsty. I walked across the soft carpet, back to the front door facing the lake, and out onto the porch. I could hear the children giggling in another room when Katherine and I said goodbye.

As I walked down the sidewalk leading to the path around the lake, I looked around for Star. I found him at the end of the Wilson's dock sitting on a bench. All the way back to our house, I told Star about the house, the kids, Katherine, and how much an hour Katherine would pay which is way more than I ever earned an hour at the Red Owl. Star got this big smile on his face like he couldn't believe our luck. Me, getting a job on the same day we moved. I couldn't believe it either. We ripped the sheets off the line when we got back to our little brown house, put them on our bed and used them right a way. If you know what I mean.

When I got up the next morning, Star was gone. A small corner bathroom had a shower and rusty sink where I brushed my teeth, washed my hair and tried to get clean with a dried up cake of soap. Star had gotten a few groceries when he brought the chicken home, so I grabbed a slice of white bread and some peanut butter to make myself a quick sandwich. A small clock hummed over the sink. It said 8:30. I figured it would take about 20 minutes to walk to Katherine's house, so I started out. Star had probably already left for work.

The day went pretty good. Katherine covered a whole bunch of things. Like, the food cans should be placed in the cupboard with the labels out so she knew what they were. When I vacuumed, the chairs should be moved—don't just vacuum around things. The kitchen should be swept after the dog ate. Always wipe out the sink when dishes are done. Check for spots on the silverware and glasses. Things like that. I felt I could handle everything the way she wanted it. She smiled a lot and said my name whenever she talked to me. When lunch time came, I was starved. Tuna with celery, pickles and mayonnaise. The tuna was white. I had never seen any like it before. Mel and I always ate tuna that was dark, and I wondered if it would taste the same. It tasted better. The bread was 7-grain. Mel and I always ate white. I liked the bread better, too. After the sandwiches, Katherine set chocolate-chocolate-chip cookies on the table—a whole plate of them. I ate only one and wanted to take one home to Star. I had tasted nothing so sweet in all my life. I could at least tell Star about it. Maybe next time, I would ask Katherine if I could just eat my cookie later and then I could give it to Star.

Katherine paid me at the end of one week. I made just as much money as I had working a week at Red Owl grocery store and deli. Star and I needed a lot of things. Food and cleaning supplies mainly. The bathroom needed shampoo and a new bar of soap. We needed laundry soap to wash our clothes even though I did it by hand. I held the check tightly as I walked home that afternoon—also looking forward to taking a ride in Star's pickup and maybe eating out.

Star never came home.

Star, God and Me

I cleaned up a bit when I got home and put on an outfit that Star liked—a sundress from the dollar store with some frilly stuff around the skirt. I pulled my hair back but let a few curls fall down next to my face and put on some pink lipstick. I waited at the wooden kitchen table; I waited outside; I waited by the lake. I even walked down the dirt road a ways in hopes to meet him on his way home. I was hungry and getting a little mad and a little worried. At sunset, I went back into our little brown house and took a good look inside the refrigerator. A half a glass of milk and a jelly sandwich would have to do. I was too tired to mix up the hamburger helper we had taken from Mel's, and besides, we had no hamburger or meat of any kind for that matter.

Sitting down at the table with my supper, I picked up the newspaper. The one that Star had brought home with Katherine's ad torn out of it. Looking through it page by page, I saw something interesting. It said FREE COUNTRY FAIR. Mel and I had always tried to get to the fair every summer when it came. According to the paper, there would be a horseshoe contest; horse, pony and rabbit judging; a derby; a queen contest and more. There would be free watermelon on Saturday afternoon and a dance that night. I wanted to go! I could hardly wait to ask Star. Plus, we had money, now. We could ride some rides and go to the dance.

Looking for other good things in the paper, a name jumped out at me in another section: Stanley Johnson. Stanley's name was listed under Magistrate-Court for disorderly conduct and writing bad checks. Who is this guy, I thought and why do people think Star is Stanley? I'd have to ask Star. Maybe he was a cousin. There were a lot of Johnson's in the world.

Putting on an old t-shirt, I thought about going to bed. The excitement over the fair was disappearing and I was very tired. Probably because the little brown house was so warm, I walked out the front door and up the path to the lake. The night air was cool and full of fireflies. Lights twinkled from the houses on the opposite shores. I felt very alone and a heaviness in my heart settled in. But, then, I looked up at the sky with its trillions of sparkly stars and felt very close to God. Right at that moment—it just came over me. I hadn't been thinking about God, but God must have been thinking about me. I no longer felt alone. "Our Father who art in heaven...." I said and got on my knees for I knew I was a child of God wherever I was—living with Star, being alone, being without Mel, in or out of church—God was with me. And this made me feel better.

Finishing the Lord's Prayer and cooling off my feet in the lake waters, I walked back to the house slow-like thinking that I could not count on Star to make me happy or even to be at my side when I was lonely. I was no longer living with my mom; I no longer had my friends from the Red owl; I could not even get to my church. I would have to find my way on my own—of course, with God right beside me. I said a *help me God*, crawled into our bed and fell into a nice sleep.

The next day was a Saturday. After another jelly sandwich, I found some paper and wrote Mel a letter. I knew Katherine would mail it for me; I could also use her address so Mel could write back. I tried to sound like everything was ok. Here's what I wrote.

Saturday morning

Hi Mom,

It's me Ledea. I hope you got my note. I would have liked to have seen you before I left but Star was in a hurry. We are living in a little brown shingled house by a lake. It took us about two hours to get here so I'm not close to you. I have some good news—I already have a job—working for Katherine Wilson. The pay is good and she is a beautiful lady who lives in a fancy house on the other side of the lake. I miss the people at the grocery store. You can tell them that for me if you would. I miss you, too, but I am ok.

Love,

Ledea, your daughter

It was still early morning when I finished the letter. Putting on my sundress again still hoping for Star to come home and maybe a chance to go to the fair, I went outside. The clouds were dark and thick and running with the wind, and lightening struck in the sky—but far off. A cool breeze lifted my dress and my hair. Walking to the lake, I made the birds to hurry on their way. The waves were higher and made bigger splashing sounds. I stopped and listened and looked—carefully. From this one spot I could see no houses, no telephone or electrical wires, just nature. The clouds, the lake, animals, the breeze, the coming storm. And I thought: this is what it must have been like when the Indians lived here. Something light gently touched my leg and looking down, I noticed a brown feather with black stripes floating next to my feet. I picked it up, dried it on my dress and stuck it behind my ear. Feeling like an Indian maiden, I named myself Lake Princess.

I waited until the rain started falling and the thunder boomed and only then returned to the little brown house. I was still Ledea, but as of that day, I was also someone else. During my alone times or during the middle of the night or while walking to and from Katherine's, I would sometimes get out the brown feather with black stripes and become the Lake Princess. There are things you can discover especially when you are alone. Some turn out to be wonderful; some are not.

I not only discovered the Lake Princess while Star was gone that time, I cleaned out my bag I had packed to move and found my Bible. I placed the Bible on the kitchen table and the transistor radio headphones on my head. 95.5 was what Pastor had set it on: KJCY— Jesus Cares For You. I heard the news and weather, songs of praise, and a message or two from some famous pastors. I walked around with a smile on my face. How did Pastor Simmons know how much this would mean to me? I felt connected to a world I had lost. So, I figured I had two good things happen to me that Saturday. One—

I discovered The Lake Princess. Two—I found my Bible and remembered my little radio from Pastor Simmons.

Star didn't come home on Saturday or Sunday morning either. I listened to the radio while doing a few house chores, then stuck the feather behind my ear and headed to the lake real quiet like. You won't believe this next story. It's a fish story. You know what they say about those. Anyway, I didn't plan this, but while I was standing in the lake water, ankle deep, this fish touched my ankles. I thought "wow." Then, I thought "wow" again—like I should catch this fish and eat it. So I reached down with both hands and scooped it up. Being slippery and all, it slipped out of my hands, but flipped itself up onto the bank and then of course, ran out of air. I felt kind of sorry for it, but I was hungry.

After washing it, I stuck the whole thing in the oven for about a half hour and then had bread and fish. I kept the feather in my hair the whole time. While I was cleaning up, I heard Star's pickup coming down the road. He walked in the house like nothing had happened. I looked at him—expecting some kind of explanation for being gone for so long. He looked at me like *why you lookin' me?* He finally asked what we had to eat.

"Star, we have no food in the house."

"Smells like food to me."

"Well, you won't believe this, but I caught a fish and ate it. I was hungry. It's gone. We'll need to get groceries. I got paid...."

"Good girl," he cut me off. "Where's the money—cash or check?" He didn't seem to be impressed by the fact that I *caught* a fish.

"Katherine wrote me a check. Can we get groceries? We need other things, too."

"Hon—ey, I need to sleep. Maybe later." He took the check from me and headed to our bed, took off his clothes and was asleep in minutes snoring, like real loud.

It was 5 o' clock in the afternoon. I crawled into bed with Star. I had missed him. I had been alone a lot. I stared at his sleeping face and wondered where he had been. He needed a shower and a shave. There were some scratches on his face I had not noticed when he first came home. I fell asleep curled up beside him.

Around 8 o'clock, I heard someone banging on our door.

"Star, someone's here!" I was afraid. Someone was trying to beat our door in.

"Who?" He asked with his eyes still closed.

And, before I could answer, four men walked into our house. They weren't any cleaner than Star, and they brought a smell with them. They talked a little funny—their words running together. It reminded me of the way those boys talked the night Maria and I made the bad decision to get into their car—the night of the horrible accident.

"Hey, Star, who you got here with you?" One of them asked. I looked around not realizing they were talking about me. By this time, Star was sitting on the edge of the bed, rubbing his eyes, but seeming not to be too surprised that four men just walked into our house without us asking them to.

"Never mind who she is. Beggars can't be choosers. What you guys doin' here anyway?"

"Star. You owe us, remember?" another one of them said—real serious like. He was standing with his feet spread wide and his arms crossed—a mean look on his face.

"Cool it, Cooper. This is a dog-eat-dog world and I ain't got nothin' for ya. If that's what you're here for, you can just get out."

"Naw, naw—settle down, Star. Next time. Gotta any booze?" Cooper asked and relaxed a little.

"Ain't got nothin' here—not even food. You guys just git."

I was getting a little worried—mainly because Star seemed to be getting a little worried. He didn't usually look or act like this. Star sat up and kind of talked them out the door. When things quieted down, I had some questions for Star. Like—who were those guys? Why were they here? How did they know where you lived? Star said that none of this was important. It was a bad time for me to be asking about Stanley Johnson's name being in the paper—I'd have to do that later.

"Star," I tried. "The fair's in town. Can we go? It's free."

Star explained that he wasn't feeling too hot, not a good time to be out and about and other excuses. If I had my real driver's license, I would've gone on my own. I was so eager to go some where, have some fun and just be around other people. As I watched Star crawl back into bed, my mind was asking me bad questions. Like, *Ledea, why did you marry Star?* When he started to do the snore thing again, I went into the kitchen, turned on the little black and white TV and watched the Hee-Haw show. The people on TV thought it was funny. I had nothing to laugh about.

Katherine Wilson

I looked forward each day to going to work for Katherine. I know you're not going to believe this, but over a period of time Katherine became my best friend. We talked about a lot of stuff. We even shared our faith in God. She invited me to come to her Bible study; they were studying James. It was held at her house making it really easy for me. Instead of going home after work, I stayed, helped Katherine with the refreshments, and then had Bible study with the group.

There were six of us, and we were of all ages and sizes. You're not going to believe this either, but I fit right in. Selma was 75 and had poor eyesight; she always asked me to read for her when it was her turn. Ruth didn't need to read from the Bible; she knew it by heart. This is exaggerating a little, but not a lot. She was 85 and filled with love; you could see it on her face and hear it in her voice. Colleen was Katherine's next door neighbor, who had her own art shop. She led the study and was good about keeping us on task. Sarah was a young mother with three children who always seemed to be late and watching the clock, but she was glad to be there — she told us so. And, then, of course, Katherine and me. We each brought our Bibles, a study book, and a pencil. We began with a prayer, used our study guide and read from the Bible and ended with a prayer. Sometimes, we prayed for each other and our loved ones. We called ourselves sisters in Christ. I never had a sister, so there were lots of reasons that Bible study made me feel special.

If you remember, I wrote Mel a letter. Well, she wrote back that she missed me, wished me the best, all that, but she also gave Katherine's address to Pastor Simmons who wrote me. Boy, was I surprised to get a letter from him. The interesting thing was that he remembered that he had given me a Bible. He wrote, *Start with James, Ledea. May you grow closer to Jesus Christ, your Lord and Savior.* And, here I was in a Bible study with a whole group of women studying James. Pastor Simmons would smile at this. A coincidence, I think, is what you call it. Or Pastor Simmons might say, "Part of God's plan, Ledea."

And, you know, I think it was part of God's plan. If you read the first few verses of James, you can see why. James starts out verse 1 by saying "Greeting." Cool, uh? Like we would say "Hi," today. Then he goes on to say, *Count it all joy, my brethren, when you meet various trials, for you know that the testing of your faith produces steadfastness. And let steadfastness have its full effect that you may be perfect and complete lacking nothing.*

The way Colleen explained this is that we can be full of joy when not so good things happen to us. Because....when this happens, our faith in God is tested. And if we stay strong, then we become steadfast—another word for endurance—which basically means you can take whatever comes along and remain strong in Christ. Mostly, because he is always there with you—something tied into grace. Another whole topic—Colleen said, and the group smiled at this.

The Bible study added another whole part to my life in several ways: one afternoon a week was filled up, Katherine and I had more to talk about than the usual stuff, and I had homework to do at our little brown house—preparing for the next lesson. Sometimes I didn't understand the questions; sometimes I didn't understand what the Bible, God's word, was trying to tell me. No one in Bible study ever made me feel stupid. One thing Colleen often said was, "Let's learn together; let's see what the study guide has to say about this."

One morning Katherine and I were baking cookies while her children were playing a board game at the kitchen table. Something like Shoots and Ladders.

"Ledea," she said kind of quiet-like and careful. "I think God brought you into my life for a purpose. I'm not sure what that is. But, I'm glad he did and if there is any way I can help you, please let me know."

I saw something in Katherine's eyes—like she knew something I didn't know. I just said a thank you and stared at her for a while. When I left that day, she sent a plate of cookies and some leftovers saying her refrigerator was too full, plus they were going to be gone —so didn't need them. I felt like Christmas walking home with a basket of goodies. I carefully put the leftovers in the refrigerator and the cookies on a cupboard shelf. Star brought food home once in a while. I couldn't always tell where he had gotten it.   It sometimes looked like someone else's leftovers. I guess he figured I didn't need much being so skinny and all.

One morning while drinking lemonade on Katherine's porch, she shared things about her life. Her dad had left her and her mom when she was three years old. Her mom later remarried, and she had two step-brothers. She said her step-dad was a good man, a Christian, but that she always wondered why her real dad left.   I felt I had something in common with Katherine as my dad left Mel and me—although way before I was three years old. After having her own children, she told me, she could never imagine being able to leave them. She felt lucky that she was also married to a man who felt the same way. Although Katherine's husband, Will, had to travel for his work, he was always home on weekends and called them daily.

She never talked much about Will, but I saw the love in her eyes when she did. With Will being gone a lot I started to convince myself that it was ok that Star was gone a lot, too. It's just what he had to do for his job. Instead of feeling bad about it, I would ask Star about it and try to give more support. Maybe Star didn't like being gone so much anymore than I liked having him be gone.

The Lake Princess

Some say that a husband and wife should share everything. I thought about telling Star about me being the Lake Princess. I would start by asking him about his job—where he went, what he did, why he had to be gone so much, how much he earned—that kind of thing. Star had never brought it up much himself, but he did like to talk about himself, so I brought it up. About once a week he brought home chicken —dark meat, lots of gravy—it always brought back memories of the Red Owl although now that I worked for Katherine, I can't really say I missed it. Star was shoveling down the potatoes, when I looked at him wondering where to start.

"Penny for your thoughts, hon—ey."

"What?"

"Penny—never mind—what's on your mind. Why you starin' at me?"

"What do you do? For work, I mean. You're gone so much."

He looked at me like he was seeing a different me. "Now, hon-ey, don't bite off more than you can chew." I looked at my food. It was almost gone.

"What do you do when you go to work and where do you go?"

"Construction, told you before." He smiled now.

"You mean, like building houses, road work; I don't know."

"Well, construction can mean lots of things, hon-ey."

"What does it mean, then? Who do you work for?"

"Self-employed. I ain't gonna take a back seat to no-one. I've survived this long doin' a little bit of this and a little bit of that, just trust me Ledea." His face said drop-it and so I did. We always had enough to get by it seemed. Although the clothes I had brought with me were hanging a little extra loose, there was always something to eat in the house—even though it might have been just bread and peanut butter.

"Star?" I still wanted to tell him about the Lake Princess.

"What you yappin' about now? A man needs a little peace. You're always tryin' to rock the boat." He had already planted himself on the lumpy couch and was clicking away at the TV channels.

"Fuzz. Fuzz. That's all we git. Darn thing."

Since Star didn't feel much like talking anymore, I decided to keep the Lake Princess a secret, and it's a good thing.

Several days later, I woke during the middle of the night. Although Star and I had gone to bed together, his side of the bed was empty. It had happened before. I was growing kind of used to it. But on this particular night, I could not go back to sleep. Eyes wide open. So, I got up and snooped. Star's black cowboy boots were inside the door and his black cowboy hat was hanging on the hook above them. I pictured him outside in his underwear. Yikes! Star just didn't go out without his boots and hat. Going back to his side of the bed, I saw that his black pants, shirt, and belt with the big silvery buckle were gone. From here, like I said, feeling snoopy, I went to the window by the front door and saw his pickup. Still there. Sitting with the moonlight reflecting off its headlights like two big eyeballs checkin' out our house. A little spooky, I thought, but at least I could tell Star was not inside his truck.

I went back to my side of the bed and pulled open the little drawer of the bed stand. Clear in the back behind my underwear was where I kept it. The feather that turned me into the Lake Princess. Pulling my hair back and holding it with a rubber band, I stuck the feather in my ponytail and quietly left the house heading for the lake. Now, I had done this before on nights when Star never came home. I would watch the stars, find the moon, study the night clouds, feel the breezes and take in the night sounds. Sometimes, I would walk part way around the lake and look at the fancy houses with their night lights reflecting off the lake and imagine what it would be like to live in one. Other times, I would just study the lake. It looked different at night. Once I saw a rowboat with two people in it talking softly. They didn't see me; I think they were in love. Another time, I sat beside the lake, feeling the cool sand beneath me and listening to the "lap, lap," of waves hitting the shoreline.

I liked silence—the kind that lets me think. It's hard to explain but let me try. During these quiet times, I was discovering things about myself. Remembering the important people in my life, like Mel, Maria, Pastor Simmons, Ms.Stenzel, Star, Katherine and even others who had not treated me so good, helped me understand me. And, I also thought a lot about God. It's pretty hard not to when you're right in the middle of nature and all God created. I would remember the Bible verse that I loved as a child—the one about the secret--"Christ is in me." And I would ask myself, "Ledea, why are you here?" "Why did God create you?" Becoming the Lake Princess helped me become closer to God. Lake Princess? Ledea? Child of Mel? Wife of Star? Friend of Katherine? Child of God? I was all this. I was a mystery.

But tonight was different, Star was out there somewhere. If I could find him, I would tell him about the Lake Princess and what she meant to me. He could be the Lake Prince. We could play the game together, and it would bring us closer. Things hadn't exactly been warm and friendly lately. Most of the time Star seemed a little mad that I was even around. So I started around the lake towards Katherine's house because that was the route I knew the best. Being barefoot, I could move without a sound. I used my eyes and ears and knew that the wind carried sounds. Grasses along the path had grown in some places to be as tall as me. I could still see through them. Music came from a bedroom window, a small light came from another. Two teenagers were sitting alongside the lake shore. I heard them before I saw them. There were no words, just sounds, and I guess *sitting* is not the word. I kept going.

There was a house that was just as large as Katherine's down the road from hers. It had a balcony on the top floor and a porch on the bottom. Again, I could hear things before I saw them. Sounds. Moving sounds. I can not explain them. The kind of sounds that let you know that something is going on even though you don't see it. And, then I saw them. One, two, three, four—I counted—persons dressed in dark clothes moving all over the house. Inside, outside, carrying things, moving things—like they were moving in the middle of the night except there were no lights. I stopped in my tracks, got down on my knees, pulled the grasses back and watched. A TV left the house carried by two of the men. Some boxes followed carried by others. In and out. Over and over. And, then, the moonlight caught something and my heart did a sommersault. The large buckle on Star's belt. I had never seen anyone else wear one like it.

Turning, I ran all the way back to our little brown house hoping and hoping that Star would be there. The house was empty. Star wouldn't go out without his hats and boots. Returning the feather to the drawer, I went from window to window in the small house looking out, looking for him. Filled with worry, I got out my Bible and Bible study lesson just to get my mind on something else. Turning on a little lamp by the kitchen table I read the name of the chapter: "Christian Faith is Tested." The opening prayer read, *Dear Lord, give me wisdom. Help me know when I should talk and when I should be still. I want wisdom that will make me usable for Your purposes. For Jesus sake. Amen.* (Friendship Bible Coffees, Stonecroft, Inc. Kansas City, Missouri) Question 2 was "What should we do if we lack wisdom for any situation?" The answer was in James 1:5. The fourth question was, "For what situation do you need special wisdom today?" I could not possibly write down my answer to this question and share it with the Bible study group. This was so big. And, yet, why did I think evil of Star? Confused, I placed my head on my arms and fell asleep.

I awoke feeling cranky and achy, but the sun was on my face coming through the tiny window above the kitchen sink. I heard Star before I saw him—snoring from the bedroom. I didn't know whether to feel better or not. He was home. I went to the door to go to the lake as I often did in the early morning. That's when I saw them. Muddy tennis shoes placed besides Star's boots. I had never seen them before. I had a lot of questions for Star. The first one would be: Whose shoes are those?

Junior

Looking at the early morning sky and listening to lake sounds made me feel better. I said the *Our Father who art in heaven* because I didn't know what to pray for. There were too many things to sort out, and I was beginning to think I didn't know Star at all. I would ask him about the tennis shoes and where he had been during the night. At least, that was the plan. All that changed when I returned to the little brown house.

There were four extra people in our house when I returned. I heard them before I even opened the back door. Lots of laughing and rough words. I quietly opened the door, stepped in, and then closed it behind me and just stood there taking it all in. The sweet smoky smell that was in our house when we moved in was back. Three of the men and Star had funny looking cigarettes, either puffing on them or holding them as the smoke drifted into their faces. Star was sitting on the edge of the bed and the guys had pulled up chairs or were standing around him. I heard the words "loot," "what a haul," stuff like that and every once in a while they would give each other the high five thing—you know with their hands up. One of the guys, the guy without the funny smelling cigarette, stood like a guard by the door as if he were not really a part of the group. I felt like a stranger in my own house. I couldn't very well turn around and walk out again. This guy with long, stringy hair and no cigarette was not only watching Star and his friends, but he had his eyes on me. So, I walked to the kitchen table, pulled out a chair—that's when they all turned and looked at me.

"Ledea, where you been, hon-ey," Star asked with a surprised look on his face—like *what you doin' here?*

"By the lake. Anybody need breakfast?" Now, I don't know where that question came from. It's not what I planned to say. It just popped out without my permission. I went to the refrigerator and got out a dozen eggs and the only loaf of bread we had. I knew how to make scrambled eggs really good. Mel always said it was my specialty. While the eggs were cooking real slow like—that's when they're the best—I popped the bread in our old toaster and then put the margarine on it.

"Come and eat," I announced like a person who was used to strangers coming for breakfast.

They all dug in and ate like they hadn't eaten for weeks. I watched them thinking I'd eat later and felt someone watching me. It wasn't Star. It was the guy who wasn't smoking with the rest; the guy with the long, stringy hair; the guy who seemed to be checking everyone else out but still eating my scrambled eggs. They called him Junior. He had these real dark eyes— almost scary. He was skinny, but strong. I noticed his muscles when he ate with his elbows on the table. Wherever I went, his eyes followed. I thought about leaving the house as I was feeling a little scared. When these men finally left, Junior was the last one out the door.

"Hey, Star, who's your woman?" is what he said to Star while looking right at me.

"Woman? Oh, Ledea, you mean. Hands off. She's with me."

Junior reached out his hand to shake mine-- like a real gentleman. He shook my hand with both of his hands holding it a little bit too long. The red started to creep up in my face. I could feel it.

"You're a lucky man, Star." Junior said while looking at me. I thought Star might get a little mad at all this, but he must have had stuff in his head because he didn't seem to be aware of the way Junior was acting.

"Yea, get out of here, Junior. Check ya out later." Star closed the door behind him. My mind was so filled with Junior's eyes and words that I forgot about the muddy shoes I wanted to ask Star about. Star went back to bed and I might have forgotten about Junior—sooner or later—if he hadn't shown up when and where he did.

When Star got up later that day, he was in a pretty good mood. He even suggested we go out to eat. "Dress up, Ledea, we're celebratin'."

"What's to celebrate?" I asked.

"We're sittin' pretty, right now, so let's enjoy it."

We filled the pickup with gas at the lake store and took off for Milville—about 20 miles down the road in a direction I hadn't been before. There were cornfields and bean fields all swaying with the wind. It felt good to be riding with the windows down in the early evening. We stopped at a Perkins. Star had a t-bone steak with hash browns and Texas toast. Since I had missed out on the scrambled eggs that morning, I ordered a big breakfast. You can get it all day long at Perkins. What a deal. I had an omelet. The waitress recommended it saying it was a step-up from scrambled eggs. It came with pancakes and bacon. The cheese oozed out of it. It was the most delightful thing I had ever eaten, and I told Star I needed to make omelets at home.

Star wanted to stop on the way home saying the one-eyed snake was restless. By now, I had figured out the one-eyed snake thing. He pulled off into a field. At that moment I was glad I had never told Star about the Lake Princess. It was a part of me that belonged only to

106

me. When we got home, Star went straight to bed. I had dressed up in my one sun-dress although the night was cool. I looked into our stained mirror over the kitchen sink and wondered if anyone thought I was pretty. Even though Star and I were married, I was lonely. I knew Star needed me in some way and he usually treated me good. But, I also felt that he really didn't know me nor did he want to. For Star, life was about Star. If someone were a part of his life, you were just that, a "part."   I would *never* be able to tell Star about the Lake Princess.

Going to the night stand, quietly opening the drawer, I pulled the brown feather with black stripes out and stuck it in my pony tail. I left the house through the back door and headed toward the lake. What I did next, I shouldn't have done. But, I did. I didn't really have time to think about it. It just happened.

Going to the lake, I kicked off my sandals and walked in. It was cool. Something caught my attention several feel away. At first I thought it was a huge silver fish floating on top of the water and then realized it was a canoe. A canoe with a man paddling it. *Junior.* I kept looking at him and he kept looking at me like we couldn't believe we were alone in the middle of the night.

He said, "Come on aboard, Ledea." He said my name so soft and sweet it was like being hypnotized. Although I was crazy scared, I let Junior help me into the somewhat tipsy boat, and we paddled all over the lake. Junior did most of the talking. He talked slow and easy about how he loved the lake, how he loved the peacefulness and stillness at night. In a short period of time, I felt closer to Junior than I ever had to Star. It was kind of soul-talk; I don't know how else to explain it. And then he said, "Tell me about yourself, Ledea."

I didn't know where to begin. No one had asked me that before. Once I got started, I had stuff to say. Stuff about my mom, my dad, Pastor Simmons, Ms Stenzel and even the accident Maria and I had been in. Junior looked at me in a way that said *I already knew all that Ledea*. It was a little strange.

"And, Star, how did you meet him?" Junior asked.

I told him about working at the Red Owl and how Star would come in and ask for chicken, dark, and lots of gravy. We both laughed. After that, it got real quiet and this funny feeling was growing in the pit of my stomach. I wanted it to go away and yet I didn't. I looked around. I didn't recognize anything. I had never been around this part of the lake before.

"Where are we?" I asked. "I need to go home."

"Home?" Junior asked like I had asked for something unusual.

"Yes. I need to go home."

Junior stopped rowing and placed one of his hands on my knee. His eyes turned dark.

"Home," I repeated. My heart was banging around in my chest so loud I thought Junior could hear it. Here I was a married woman out in the middle of the night in the middle of a lake with someone I barely knew.

"Home," he repeated and picked up the oars. I turned my back to him the rest of the way home and pretended to look at the scenery—although at night there wasn't much to see. He paddled the canoe up to our bank and hopped out to help me. Before I could walk around him to get to our house, his arms were around me and his hands in my hair. I'm sure he could feel my heart doing something like jumping jacks inside my chest.

He pulled the feather from my hair and asked, "What's this, Ledea?"

"Just a feather. I found it." Like it was any of his business.

He carefully placed it behind my ear and this part you won't believe. He said, "You look just like a princess, a Lake Princess."

My eyes almost popped out of my head. Backing away slowing, I left Junior standing by the lake. As I closed the little brown house door behind me, I saw him standing at the lake shore with the moon behind him and the canoe beside him. Junior stood there like a statute and then lifted his hand in a slow wave—the kind you see in parades.

Lake Princess

You might be thinking, Ledea just had a chapter about the Lake Princess. Is this a mistake? It's not. There's more and it gets a little scary. I sort of forgot about the muddy shoes. The stuff about Junior—I couldn't stop thinking about him. Was he a bad person or not? He almost seemed gentle, and the look in his eyes was pretty much burned in my brain. I could not stop thinking about that. So, I went to work the next few days like nothing was different. However, the first day I walked to Katherine's after all this happened, I noticed the canoe was still in the lake outside our house. Just sitting there empty. Same the next day and the next. In fact, it sat there the whole week bouncing in the water like it was lost. Maybe Junior had borrowed it and not returned it. Maybe it was his and he was just leaving it here because he had no place to keep it. Anyway, it was kind of a mystery and also became a temptation to me. I finally decided to ask Star about it.

"Whose canoe up by the lake?" I asked him one afternoon when we both just happened to be home at the same time—pretending I knew nothing about it.

"Who knows." Star didn't seem to be even curious.

"Why would someone leave their canoe here, Star?" I asked trying to see if he knew anything about Junior.

"It's just a canoe, Ledea. It ain't like we got a speed boat out there just waitin' for us to hop in and take off. You gotta paddle it."

"But..."

"Somebody will pick it up. And if they don't, we'll sell it in a few weeks. No skin off my nose."

I had given up trying to understand a lot of what Star said. But it seemed to me that Star didn't have much interest in the canoe and didn't know where it came from. Being the Lake Princess and all, I started to make plans. Indians had canoes; maybe not like this one, but I had a good imagination. So, one of those nights several weeks later when I could not sleep, I slipped the feather into my hair and headed toward the lake. There it was bobbin' in the water, just waiting for me.

It was a different kind of night. The moon was like a big light bulb in the sky, but spidery clouds kept drifting through it. Everything was still. No wind. I could hear sounds from all over the lake but not tell where they were really coming from. Kids playing tag— *You're it—No, you're it!* Some adults talking and laughing in another area. … *remember the fish story…* Stuff like that. Kind of spooky and yet kind of a comfort. Voices and not knowing where exactly they were coming from or who.

I walked in the cool water up to my ankles and then to my knees before carefully stepping into the canoe. I took the oars and pushed off the ground to get out of the grasses along the shoreline. And, then, I paddled. I had watched Junior closely that night, so I knew what to do. Soon enough, I was in the middle of the lake. The lake was black and smooth, and I was just gliding across it feeling like a real Indian princess when the moon came out big and bold. No more clouds covering it. Moon beams shot across the water and there I was picture perfect—rowing in the moonlight. At first,

I thought this was a good sign. It was ok to take the canoe and do this in the middle of the night because it was all so beautiful and peaceful. Then the bad stuff started happening.

The voices I had heard earlier were louder. I heard a motor start up—one of those speed boat motors—big and loud and powerful. The moonlight was no longer a good thing. Someone had spotted me on the lake. And, they were headed for me. I kept saying to myself, "Ledea, you are so stupid; Ledea you are so stupid," as I tried to turn the boat and get out of the moonlight. As the light from the boat came closer and closer, I knew I could not out-paddle this monster, so I slid over the side of the canoe and into the water just as the light from the motor boat hit the canoe.

Katherine had taught me a few strokes when we swam with her children, but I was especially good at something she called treading. So by this time I was not scared to be in deep water. However, I was scared of the big boat still coming. I hid on the backside of the canoe and planned on going under the water to the other side if I had to—if the speed boat circled my canoe. My heart was racing and I was breathing real hard kind of like a dog pants after chasing a squirrel. I was afraid they would hear me but then realized as the boat got even closer that my breathing would not be louder than this boat motor roaring in the middle of the night. Right next to my canoe, they stopped, and the waves washed over me. Voices. Men's voices.

"What in tarnation this boat doin' out in the middle of the lake?" One of them said.

"Suppose someone drown*ded*?" Another one asked. They all laughed at this. Like it would be funny.

"It's just a stupid canoe. Who wants it? Been sittin' at my place for a week now. Dime a dozen." My heart stopped. Star. My first thought was to show myself. Star could get me back home safely. My second thought—which came right away—was *no, Ledea, stay put*. While they laughed and circled my canoe slowly as I bobbed from one side to the other, I realized again how much I didn't know about Star, what he did, how he spent his time and who he hung out with.

Bored, they soon left. I knew I could not go back to our house with this canoe. A boat doesn't find its own way back. So, I paddled to Katherine's dock and attached it to an end post. I would tell her about it tomorrow. Dripping wet, nervous and cold, I ran like a wild woman all the way home—hoping to get there before Star.

God

Why do we always forget God until we REALLY need him? I said the Lord's Prayer all the way home, especially the "forgive us our trespasses" and the "lead us not into temptation" parts. I tried to remember some of the Bible verses and songs I had memorized as a child, but the only thing that I could remember was "washed in his blood"—probably because I was soaking wet. When I reached our little house, there were no lights on. Real quiet-like, I opened the lakeside door and slipped in. Star always snored loudly, and there was no snoring, so I thought I was safe. Right away—I dropped all my wet stuff on the floor and left them in a pile and headed for our bed to find my PJs. I say PJs, but actually the PJs were just a t-shirt and shorts I always wore to bed. I usually stick them under my pillow. Feeling around—I felt a body. Star! I screamed—not just because I hadn't expected him to be there but also because he was wide awake and looking right at me!

He grabbed me quick like and said, "Ledea, are you off your rocker? Where you been?"

I was never good at lying. Even if I had to—I would have trouble coming up with a good lie. It just wasn't in me. So I answered, "In the lake, Star. I'm freezing."

"Lake? This time of night? Nutty as a fruitcake with a screw loose to top it off. What did I get myself into?"

"What *did* you get yourself into?" I asked Star. I didn't mean to be funny, but Star thought it was. Anyway, he laughed and I did, too—a scared kind of laugh. He fell asleep that way—holding me close. When the snoring started, I put my PJs on and climbed back into bed. I couldn't go to sleep. Maybe it was a good thing as that's when one of the Bible verses came back to me—you'll remember it, too. *The Lord is my helper. I will not be afraid. What can man do to me?*

I kept telling myself I didn't need to be afraid of Star, Junior, or maybe, even myself. I did need to trust in God. I had been paying attention to way too many other things lately.

The following morning, after Star and I ate cornflakes together, I got out my Bible study materials—the booklet on James and my Bible. And right in front of Star I read the first part of James again. *Count it all joy, my brethren, when you meet various trials for you know that the testing of your faith produces steadfastness. …. And if any of you lacks wisdom, let him ask God…."* I was pretty much figuring out that God might be trying to get my attention.

Star stared at me kind of angry like and said, "Give me that."

I handed the Bible to him with it open to James. He looked at it—scratching his head.

"Where'd you learn to read like that?" he said angry-like.

"Star, I went to school." That's what kids do in school—learn to read.

"Here, I thought…. Never mind." And with that Star dropped the Bible on the table and stomped out of the room. I started to think that Star didn't know how to read. At least, not the harder words like you find in the Bible. I didn't know whether to be sad for Star or happy for me. Like I said before, maybe Star wasn't so smart after all. Or maybe, we were smart in different ways.

After that—I didn't know how to pray or what to pray for. Everything was so mixed up. Thank goodness, Katherine was my friend. But where would I start?

Katherine

I left for work the next day feeling better—like soon I would get all this stuff out of my head. Katherine could help me figure it out. But where do you start telling someone about everything wrong or funny going on in your life when you can put no sense to it yourself? Especially, when some of it was pretty bad.

There was one road that intersected the lake path on the way to Katherine's. You could hear a car coming from a mile a way, so I never looked right or left. This morning, especially, I had my eyes down. I had a lot to think about. That's the reason I saw it before stepping on it. Right in the center of that road was a frog—flat as a pancake. Soon as I thought it, I smiled. *Flat as a pancake* was something Star would say. Its insides were coming out from both ends. Gross, you're thinking. That's what I thought. *Wrong place, wrong time* was the next thing I thought. And I smiled again thinking I was starting to think too much like Star. Then my mind started asking funny questions of me, like, *Ledea, were you at the wrong place, wrong time when you met Star?* Pastor Simmons always said we should pray about everything, asking God for guidance in all things. I hadn't prayed about

Star. It all just seemed to fall into place—or into a bad place.

I heard Mel talk about fate. Meaning, I guess, that some things were just bound to happen. Did someone plan a long time ago that I was to marry Star and have all this happen, and, if so, for what reason? Where would I start with all of this with Katherine? And WHAT IF Star were actually a thief? The thought of Star being in jail made me very nervous. It also made me feel a little guilty. Would people think me bad because I was Star's wife? Could I have stopped Star if only we could have talked? The newspaper and TV always made a big deal about bad people. Would Star make the paper or TV news? Would they say he was married to me? I was ashamed to think of what Pastor Simmons, Ms. Stenzel and even those cops who said, *Star Johnson? You mean Stanley?* would think. I had been proud to be married and wanted and loved. And, look at the mess I was in. Before I reached Katherine's house, my footsteps had slowed. Maybe I didn't want to tell her. Maybe I wouldn't feel better.

So, instead of marching right into the kitchen door like most mornings, I walked to the front porch and sat on the porch swing and rocked. Back and forth, back and forth trying to think how to bring this up to Katherine. I looked out onto the clear morning lake, saw a few birds and watched the grass kind of float in the wind. That's when I missed it. My feather that turned me into the Lake Princess was somewhere out on the lake—lost the night I had to get into the water. It had been my escape, my secret, and now the Lake Princess was gone along with the feather. Strange as it may seem, that is what made me cry. So much was wrong or not understood and the lost feather is what started me crying. That is how Katherine found me.

"Ledea, what are you doing out here?" I heard her voice and then the screen door snapping shut.

"I'm sorry, Katherine. I'm late. I lost my feather."

She looked at her watch. "Well, you're only a couple of minutes late." She was looking real concerned at this point. "And, what feather are you talking about?"

"No one knows about it."

"The feather?"

"Yes. No one knows about it. Not even Star."

"It's your feather? Where did you lose it?"

"In the lake. You know the canoe at the end of the dock? It happened that night I brought the canoe."

Katherine said nothing for a while. "So...the canoe is tied in with the feather. Were you out in the canoe, Ledea?"

"Yes. That night I was. Some men saw me. I had to hide in the lake. That's when I lost it."

"I see." Katherine looked out into the lake and then into her house as if she had something she needed to take care of. "Where did the feather come from, Ledea?"

"I found it. By the lake. It was brown with black stripes."

"A pheasant feather?"

I looked up. I had always wondered what bird it came from.

"Maybe."

"Why was it so special to you?"

"When I wore it, I became the Lake Princess. No one else knew. I became someone else."

With this, she took my hand and sat beside me. We rocked together looking out onto the lake. We could hear Kendra and Kyle inside—the light sound of children talking. We sat like that for maybe five minutes.

"What else do you want to tell me?" Katherine asked still pushing her foot against the porch floor to keep the swing rocking.

She was so kind. I couldn't look at her. She had two children giggling inside the house, a husband who went to a real job every day, a house with porches and soft furniture and food in her refrigerator. I remembered the church custodian when I was a child who treated me like a germ. Katherine would never treat me anyway but in a loving way: but still, at that point, I felt like a germ, a stranger, and less than human.

"Ledea, you know what we have said about being good friends? You know you can talk to me. Is it Star?"

"I guess he's a big part of it. But along with that, I guess I miss my mom and everything I had before. You've been wonderful, but a lot has happened since I moved here…. Some of it not very good….. Some of it I don't understand."

"Where does Star work?"

"I'm not sure. When I ask him, he says stuff like construction work, self-employed. He's gone a lot and I'm never sure where he is or when he will come home. Like the other night—the night I lost the feather—Star was gone so I became the Lake Princess and went out for a canoe ride. Everything was fine until this speed boat saw me. By the time they got to me, I was in the water hiding. I recognized Star's voice. He was with them. I don't know why."

"Ledea, there's been some robberies in some of the lake homes recently. Do you suppose these men were a part of it?"

Katherine didn't ask if I thought Star was a part of it. I couldn't very easily turn in my own husband. I remembered the moon light striking the belt buckle the night I saw men robbing one of the lake houses—and thinking it could be Star.

"They might be," was as close as I could get to saying anything bad about Star.

I didn't mention the muddy shoes I found afterwards, the strange men who showed up once in a while at our house, the sweet smoky smell they always brought with them.

"What do you want me to do?" Katherine asked.

This question kind of threw me. Not knowing how to answer her, I shrugged my shoulders.

"Do you feel safe?" Katherine asked.

"I think so." I wasn't real sure what Katherine meant. Did she think someone was trying to hurt me?

"Come with me." Katherine took my hand, pulled me off the porch swing, lead me through the porch screen door, past Kyle and Kendra who were playing *Shoots and Ladders* on the floor and up the steps leading to the second floor. We walked past the bedrooms and the large bathroom to a door at the end of the hall.

"I've never shown you this part of the house. We've been too busy taking care of the rest of it. Come with me." The door creaked a little when Katherine opened it. There was another set of steps behind the door. I followed her up some wooden steps which cracked a little like they hadn't been used in a while. What I saw at the top of the stairs amazed me. Another whole house. At the very top of the stairs was a small living room with a couch, TV set and a reclining chair— all in colors matching the rug in the middle. At the other end, towards the backside of the house, was a mini-kitchen along the wall with a microwave, stove-top, small refrigerator, sink and cupboards full of a set of dishes and a few pots and pans. Between the living room and kitchen was a circular wooden table with two chairs. Katherine motioned for me to follow her past the living room again to the other end of the room. We walked through an arched doorway which lead to a small, but cozy bedroom with a large window over-looking the lake.

"Katherine, who lives here?"

"No one, right now. My mother used to live here in between her travels. We kept it for her so she'd have her own space when she wanted to visit."

"Wow." I said it quiet-like, because I didn't want Katherine to know how WOW I really thought it was. "I can't believe this was up here and I never knew about it."

"Well, you know about it now. We'll clean it today—although it won't need much."

"Sure." I looked at her—ready to start. I would be glad to be busy.

"We're cleaning it for a reason, Ledea." She stopped until I looked at her. "If you ever need a place to stay. If for some reason you don't feel safe, you can come here. No questions asked."

"No questions asked?" I didn't know for sure what she meant.

"No questions asked." She repeated and kept looking at me until she knew I got what she meant. I finally got it and nodded my head.

"Thank you," I mumbled. Katherine hugged me and from that point, I felt safer just knowing she was there for me. On my way home that day, I told myself that Jesus Christ was surely within Katherine. I smiled thinking about it.

Star

As the weeks passed, Star spent even more time away from home. When he was home, he slept a lot. Katherine let me take leftovers to the little brown house a couple times a week. If not for this, I would have starved. Star took the checks Katherine gave me.

Sometimes he brought groceries home; sometimes not. His friends showed up again—noisy as ever—bringing girlfriends with them. They were drinking straight out of whiskey bottles and then throwing them in the corners of our house. It made me sick. It was my house and I took care of it. Even though Star and I didn't have much, our house was neat and clean.

That night, Star also made me sick. I already had all these unanswered questions about muddy shoes, belt buckle in the moonlight, being gone all the time, his job, who he hung out with and how he spent my checks from Katherine. Whenever I asked him anything, which I was more apt to do, he never gave a straight answer. I ended up more confused than before. Star seemed to enjoy making me feel stupid. I did not like this about him. I was starting to think that he really did not love me or, worse yet, even care very much for me as a person.

That one night when his friends were there was the worst night of our married life. Usually when his friends were there, I would leave the house and come back when they were gone. However, on that night, with all the girlfriends being there, Star expected me to stay. He was forcing whiskey down my throat and touching me in certain places that people don't do in public. I was embarrassed and ashamed. Star didn't realize what he was doing to me or he didn't care. It was bad either way.

When I asked him to stop his grabbing, he yelled, "Let your hair down, woman. You're a stupid bump on a log."

Everyone thought it was funny and started chanting, "Ledea's a stupid bump." Someone else said, "Cheers to that," and they clinked their bottles together and laughed more. I got sick and I'm embarrassed to say it, but I threw up on Star. This really got them laughing—so hard that some of them were red in the face and bent over.

"Ledea's not only a stupid bump, she's a drunk bump," one of the women said. She was blonde with big hair, loud and taller than any of Star's friends. I hated her for saying it. Star pushed me off his lap, said some really bad words, and then pushed me into one of the corners. I hit some broken glass as I fell and threw up again. Picking myself up, I walked funny like to the back door heading for the lake. I so wanted to be the Lake Princess at that point. My feather was gone, the canoe was gone and I felt like a nothing. Washing my cut hand in the lake's water, I cried and cried and cried until there were no more tears but only hurt sounds and little whimpers. How had it gotten so bad?

Katherine had said *if you ever don't feel safe you can come here.* I could not show up at Katherine's like this: drunk, dirty, and hurt. I found a soft place in the grass, finished crying, curled up into a ball to keep warm, and listened to the waves as they softly hit the shoreline—one after another—trying not to think about everything that had just happened.

I dozed off and started dreaming. Maria was there, and she was saying *dummy, dummy, dummy.* And, I felt bad because I thought she was my friend. Mel was in a part of my dream looking confused again. Then I was a child at Pastor Simmons' feet listening to a children's sermon about how all of us were children of God. I soon felt warm and fuzzy all over. Someone was holding me gently.

I'm not sure what woke me—maybe it was the noise still coming from the house-- but I did realize that someone really *was* holding me. His body was curled around mine, and he was holding me gently. His warm breath was on my neck. I didn't want to move. Star? Star was bigger. Star had never held me this way. Not knowing whether to be afraid or not, I pretended to sleep.

"Ledea, are you awake?" A man's voice asked.

"No. I mean yes, I guess."

"Are you ok?"

"Sort of."

"What Star did was not right."

I didn't say anything.

"Let me see your hand?"

I sat up to show this gentle person my hand. It was Junior. He took a red handkerchief—the kind farmers and cowboys use—out of his pocket and wrapped it around my hand.

"You may need stitches." He studied it carefully in the moonlight.

"It'll be ok." I pulled my hand away. I was embarrassed that Junior knew what had happened to me.

"Were you in the house?" I asked him.

"No. But, I heard what happened. That's why I came." He took my cut hand in his again and gently held it.

"I'm sorry." It's all I could think of to say.

"Sorry?" Junior looked confused. I shrugged. I was hurt, drunk and a mess.

"Your hand. We need to take care of it. This cut is deep enough. You might need stitches. Will you come with me?" He was so careful with the words he used, and his look was so gentle. I would have gone with him anywhere.

Junior

I went with Junior; he took me to the hospital in his car. It took us awhile to get there and neither of us said anything. He turned on the radio. I recognized it. It was KJCY—the station Pastor Simmons had told me about—the one I listened to but not often. A man with a deep voice was saying "God cares for you—each and every one of you." Soft, beautiful music followed, "Earnestly, tenderly Jesus is calling…." With the warm air from the heater on my feet, the music, and someone who cared beside me, I felt like I was on my way to heaven even though I was drunk and hurt.

Junior paid the bill at the emergency room after talking to a tired lady behind a desk and filling out some paper work. I over-heard words like "just a friend, trying to help out," that kind of stuff. We rode all the way home listening to the same deep voice and gentle music. The car was warm, Junior took my hand in his hand, and we rode like that. It was the middle of the night, and I wanted time to stop. I wanted to feel cared for. I tried to pretend that Star was just a bad dream, that I was Junior's *woman* as Star would put it and we were on our way home. A different home; a home that belonged to Junior and me. I almost could believe it, that is, until Junior pulled into the lane that led to the little house on the lake. The little house that Star brought me to seemingly so long ago. The dirty little house with the funny smells was now the same little house but now with dirty stuff going on, dirty little secrets.

"Things should have settled down by now," Junior said stopping the car and turning the key. "Are you going to be ok?"

I said thank you thinking I was not going to be ok, but there was nothing anyone could do about it, even Junior, and climbed out of the car and headed directly to the house-- head down all the way. Staying longer in the car, having to talk to Junior, having to look at Junior would only turn me into a puddle of tears.

Me

As I walked to the house, Junior started the car, turned around and drove back down the dusty lane. It was early morning—still pretty dark. There was a heavy feeling inside my chest. I knew Star and I could not go on as before. I would have to talk to him. We could not live this way. It would not be easy--Star being Star. Star always thinking his thinking was the only way to think.

Instead of using the front door, I went around the house to the lake. I needed a plan. I would have to use my words carefully or Star would just walk away from me, stay away for several days and then come back like nothing had happened. I decided to fix breakfast for him. Maybe, he would talk with some scrambled eggs inside him.

Taking a deep breath, I opened the back door and stepped inside real quiet. It smelled of whiskey, that sweet smell from their cigarettes and body sweat. Bottles, cans, broken glass were scattered, but at least the house was empty except for Star snoring loudly from the bedroom. Not wanting to wake him, I decided to get some sleep myself before the scrambled eggs. I slipped my sandals off, carefully pulled my t-shirt off my head trying not to mess up my bandaged hand, and then I saw her. The blonde lady who said, "Ledea's not only a stupid bump; she's a drunk bump." She was next to Star in our bed, and she had no PJs on or anything else for that matter. I must have stopped breathing, because suddenly I was taking deep breaths like I had been running out of air. Taking a few steps back from the bed but keeping my eyes on Star and the naked lady, I pulled the t-shirt back over my head, slipped my sandals on, headed for the door, and left our little house in the woods.

The phrase *dirty secrets, dirty secrets, and what else don't you know, Ledea?* kept running through my head like a fast moving train along with something Star often told me, *you're not the sharpest took in the shed, Ledea.* I could not get the picture out of my head of the naked lady in my bed all the way to Katherine's. No matter how I tried, it just wouldn't go away. Seeing that the kitchen light was on, I knocked on her back door. Katherine was there in a few seconds, dressed in a yellow bathrobe, her curly red hair up in a ponytail.

"Ledea, come in. It's so early. You ok?"

'Yes. No. Not really." I was shaking like a crazy lady.

"Well you're here, now. Have some coffee with me? Are you cold?"

Even though I didn't answer, Katherine poured two cups, popped some toast in the toaster and sat down. That's when she noticed my hand.

"What happened?" Her voice was louder.

"I cut myself. Someone took me to the emergency room. Some stitches and a shot. I'll be ok—they said."

'You're sure?" I nodded. "How did it happen?"

"Star had a party. Lots of his friends came. Things got really bad. It was an accident."

Katherine buttered our toast and set the peanut butter and blueberry jelly on the table with a knife for each of us. Looking at my hand again, she took my knife and put peanut butter and jelly on some toast and cut it in four little squares.

"Eat." She said. "You must be hungry."

I didn't know if the sick feeling in my stomach was because I was hungry or because of what I had just seen. Maybe both.

We ate in silence. The warm toast and just sitting with Katherine helped me relax. The refrigerator hummed in the corner, and I could hear the washing machine in the laundry room already spinning—getting ready for the rinse cycle.
The buzzer went off on the oven, and I smelled chocolate chip muffins as Katherine took them from the oven— Kendra and Kyle's favorite.

"Do you need a place to stay?" She asked as she sat down again.

I nodded. I could not go back.

"Ok. Follow me. Let's get you settled."

Katherine showed me where the towels were and how to work the shower. She gave me a plastic bag to put over my bandaged hand and left. After showering and trying to wash my hair with one hand, I wrapped the towel around me and wondered what to do next.

"Clothes on the bed are for you, Ledea," she shouted from the second floor. "I'll meet you downstairs. On second thought, get some rest first. Come down when you're ready. We'll eventually get everything done."

I pulled on a pair of gray sweat pants and a pink t-shirt with NIKE on it. Katherine even had underwear for me; she had thought of everything. After dressing, I rested my bandaged hand on one of the pillows and fell asleep. Katherine finally woke me around lunch time.

"Ledea, you must be hungry. Come eat with us." She was at my bedside rubbing my back.

I sat up. "I'm sorry, I didn't mean to sleep so long. I'm supposed to be working today."

"We're not going to worry about work. We're going to get you settled. We'll get back to our schedule tomorrow. Right now, we need to eat. Wild rice soup and ham sandwiches. Ready?"

When I came down to the kitchen, Kyle and Kendra were wide-eyed and sitting at the table waiting for me.

"Are you going to live with us?" Kendra asked after our prayer.

I looked at Katherine.

"Ledea's staying with us for as long as she wants or needs to. She has the upstairs apartment where Grandma used to stay."

"Good!" Kyle said. "Can we visit you?"

"I'm right here, silly," I answered which made everyone laugh.

"That's Ledea place. If you want to visit her when she's upstairs, you'll have to ask her first," Katherine explained.

Neither Kyle or Kendra asked about my bandaged hand although I did see each one try to get a good look at it as I ate the hot soup and sandwich. Katherine must have told them not to ask.

As we cleaned off the table, Katherine said I looked nice in pink and told me she had a box or two of extra clothes she had out-grown since having children. She brought them upstairs after lunch and we went through them. She thought of a memory or two to each shirt, pair of jeans, or skirt she pulled from the box. I was learning more about Katherine. She had "skinny" jeans and "fat" jeans. She gave me the skinny jeans. When she left, I tried everything on—mixing and matching things—and looked in the tall mirror behind the door. I barely recognized myself and almost giggled.

Kyle brought some books up to me, showed me how to run the remote control on the TV and told me his mom said to take the rest of the day off. As I was walking around the little apartment, I thought of something. My Bible and little radio Pastor Simmons gave me were at our little house. I walked to the window overlooking the lake in my bedroom. Looking far to the left, I could see a brown spot among the trees—my house. Would Star be home? Would the naked lady be there? Should I try to get the Bible and radio? I couldn't possibly ask Katherine to go with me. She was too nice. She was too perfect. Besides the feather, which was at the bottom of the lake or lost in some weeds along the shore, my Bible and radio were my two most precious things.

Betsy

Knowing Star didn't usually spend much time at the little brown house, I thought I could go almost any time and get my things. If he was there, we would have to talk, although I was not really ready for that. I didn't go during the day, because Katherine paid me to work for her—besides, I didn't want her to know I was going. So one night later during the week, I waited until everyone was in bed and snuck out of Katherine's house and headed down the path toward the little brown house. I felt a little sneaky and not good about this because I knew Katherine would not like it—thinking it not safe. And even though it was less than a week since I had left, it all felt very strange. Maybe, because so much had happened.

The moon spent most of its time behind some dark clouds. And, to be honest, I felt kind of spooky about all of this—breaking into my own house in the middle of the night. I remembered the time I had watched the robbery in the middle of another night months ago—men dressed in black taking things and seeing what I thought was Star's belt buckle. A bunch of what-ifs were going around in my head making me feel like a big scarity cat. I walked slowly and listened very carefully wishing I had my feather. About thirty steps from the little house, I heard talking. It wasn't coming from the house; it was coming from the lake shore outside our house. Getting down on my hands and knees, I crawled through the tall grass until I could see. I saw the lake first, the waves quiet-like on the shore line. Then, there they were-- two people on a blanket next to the lake.

"She's an albatross around my neck, Betsy. Don't want nothin' to do with her anymore."

I heard smooching and other non-word sounds. I peeked through the grass again to see the lady who had been naked in my bed.

"Star, ya know I can give ya what ya need." A woman's voice said—her words slurred together and slow—kind of like when you have too much peanut butter in your mouth.

"Yea, birds of a feather, Betsy—you and me."

"What are ya goin' do?" The woman's voice again.

"Don't know yet. A rollin' stone gathers no moss. We'll come up with a plan." More smooching. "You and me, Betsy."

Crawling backwards, I got out of the tall grass and headed toward the front of the house—the door on the other side of the lake shore. Star's old pickup was sitting in its usual parking spot with the moonlight reflecting off the front windows. Like I said—spooky. I opened the front house door slowly remembering how it always made screeching noises and tiptoed through the house in the dark. Getting my Bible and radio from the little stand by the bed that used to belong to Star and me, I left the little house. It was no longer my home.

Returning to Katherine's with a heavy feeling inside I had never had before, I headed to the dock, sat on the bench and looked out at the lake. A storm was coming. The clouds were picking up speed across the night sky, and the waves grew loud and angry as they hit the shoreline one right after another. Thunder rumbled in the distance and lightening cut across the sky. The wind took a hold of me, whipping my hair across my face, and I knew it had the strength to throw me into the lake if I didn't hold on. I gripped the end of the wooden bench and dared it to do so. As the rain and wind beat against me, I screamed into the storm. I belonged to no one.

Katherine

Katherine found me the next morning—still at the end of the dock. I heard her footsteps padding down the wood planks long before her voice but was too tired and sad to look at her.

"Ledea, whatever are you doing out here? Are you ok? Look at you...."

With Katherine, it was always *are you ok*? No, I was not and I was too sad to tell her, so I said nothing and hid my face because I was ashamed at how I must look--especially with her being so beautiful.

"Ledea!" She pulled my shoulder back and I had to look at her.

"Are you ok?" she asked again. "What are you doing out here? How long have you been here? There was a storm last night! We lost some tree branches. Are you ok?"

I turned away, looked out at the lake with the early morning sun stinging my eyes, and wanted to jump in, sink to the bottom and never come up.

"Ledea, you must talk to me. Whatever it is, I can help you. Trust me. Please." I knew Katherine would not go away.

"I am not ok. Everything is wrong. Everything."

She sat on the dock beside me and said nothing for a while. Then, she softly took my hand in hers and held it on her lap.

"God doesn't allow anything to happen to us that we can not handle, Ledea. Sometimes, I think that God has put you in my life for that reason. With my husband being gone so often, you have been a dear companion to me. Please let me help you. It's my turn now."

"You've already helped me. You've given me a place to stay. A place to live. Clothes. A job." I took a deep breath. "But this, this is too big. You can not help me with this. No one can."

"At least tell me what it is. I can make the decision as to whether I can help you or not. Can you do that?"

The waves started to hit our feet as they hung off the dock. We both started to swing our legs hitting the small waves as they came at us. She squeezed my hand. I squeezed back.

"Let's go inside. Breakfast sound like a good idea?"

Standing up, she put her arm around my shoulders and we walked together to the house. The kitchen was warm and smelled of freshly brewed coffee. Katherine cut me a large square of cinnamon coffee cake still warm from the oven and sat down opposite me.

We ate in silence.

"Ledea?" was all she had to say and it all came out. Everything. Star and Betsy on the beach. Star and Betsy, naked, in our bed the night of the party. Star pushing me into the broken glass. Canoeing on the lake in the middle of the night as the Lake Princess and having to hide from the men in a motor boat. The robbery and seeing Star's belt buckle in the moonlight. The muddy shoes. Me, not understanding what Star did for a job. His loud friends who showed up at weird times. Katherine said nothing but she seemed to be thinking very hard.

Finally she asked, "Ledea, what do we need to do?"

"I don't know. Everything is wrong. Nothing is right. Why did I marry Star? I thought he loved me? This is such a mess."

"I can't answer any of those questions for you, Ledea. Let's take things one step at a time. Right now, you need to take a shower, get some clean clothes. After a short nap, we're going to get some things done around here and then plan our weekend. How would you like to visit Mel? Maybe we could take her to church on Sunday morning and I could meet this Pastor Simmons you've been telling me about."

"I would like that," I answered and felt a heaviness lifted from my chest. Katherine, somehow, thought of everything. She seemed to understand me better than Mel or Pastor Simmons or even Mrs. Stenzel. Thinking of Mel made me very homesick. It had been so long and so much had happened.

Pastor Simmons

Katherine and I sat together in my old church. Mel was in the choir grinning every time she looked at me. I hadn't told her anything—good thing—she was so happy to see me. The choir sang, "Lord of all hopefulness...."

Katherine and I had tears in our eyes and I think Mel did, too. Pastor Simmons' sermon followed about how we were God's children and that he was always there for us. Always. No matter the circumstances. Trust in him. He took care of the birds and the lilies in the field; he surely took care of me. As I sat there in the church—that same church I had gone to as a child--I wanted that faith back I had as a child. Knowing I was special in God's sight and that was enough.

As we left, Pastor Simmons shook my hand. I introduced him to Katherine.

"You are in my prayers, Ledea," he told me gently as I was thinking *if you only knew.*

"Thank you," was all I could say.

"Remember, James. Are you reading it?" He asked.

With a line-up of others behind us, I didn't take time to tell him we were studying it in our Bible study group. He would have been impressed.

Katherine, Mel and I left together. We picked up deli sandwiches, a bag of chips, and each a can of pop at the Red Owl on our way back to Mel's so we could eat together. Katherine's car looked out of place in our neighborhood, but she didn't seem to notice. Mel was always kind of quiet so Katherine did most of the talking. Telling Mel what a good worker I was, how the children enjoyed my company and how she appreciated me. She didn't mention that I was living with her. I guess she left that up to me.

"How is Star?" Mel finally asked a question.

"Star?" I asked. Kind of like *who is Star?*

"Yes, how is he?" Mel repeated.

"I'm not sure." I put my head down—not knowing how to go on. Katherine saved me and told Mel that I was going through a difficult time.

"Ledea's staying with me right now. Until things are worked out. I want you to know that she is safe; she still has a job. I hope you're ok with that."

Mel looked a little puzzled, rubbed between her eyes with the palm of her hand, and then looked out the window.

"Always wondered about that one," she finally said still looking out the window.

Katherine

Life at Katherine's house was a better life than I ever had. There were times when I felt a little guilty— thinking I did not deserve any of this—especially when I thought of Mel living in our old, worn-out neighborhood in a little gray house. Katherine treated me like a sister. We worked together during the day, she took me with her to run errands, and we played with Kyle and Kendra. Several weeks after me moving in, Katherine's husband, Will, got a different job that meant he didn't have to travel so much. We celebrated at supper that night, and I secretly wondered what this would mean for me. It ended up meaning nothing bad. In fact, it was kind of good. Will didn't treat me like a sister; he treated me more like his oldest daughter. He would often ask me, "What's up Ledea?" I would answer, "the sky," and we would both laugh. It was our little joke between the two of us. He always included me in supper table talk. Like, "What do you think, Ledea?" And, "Now, Ledea, I heard today that..." That kind of thing.

Now that Will was home, he spent more time with Kendra and Kyle which meant that Katherine had more time with just me. One day we had pedicures and manicures together. Afterwards, Katherine said there was a "Crazy Day" sale going on in the shops, and we should look for bargains. I came home with three new outfits. Plus, and you won't believe this—I got my ears pierced with little diamond-like studs. We were walking by this jewelry place and without thinking, I said to Katherine that I always wanted to get my ears pierced but Mel said we couldn't afford it. Within minutes, there they were in my ears! I probably felt a little bit like Cinderella when the pumpkin turned into a coach and all that other magic stuff happened --without the prince, of course.

I must have glowed after all this because when we got home, Kendra, Kyle and Will all said at the same time, "Wow" and "Look at Ledea!"

Katherine kiddingly said, "Hey guys, what about me?" Everyone laughed. Katherine always looked beautiful.

That night I went to bed still feeling like Cinderella. However, during the middle of the night, my ears started itching a little. I had a bottle of stuff to put on them to stop any infection, so I got up to get the cotton balls and the bottle After treating my ears, I turned off the light and went back to my bed. Sitting on the edge, I looked out the big window over-looking the lake. Everything was calm and peaceful-like. Giggling to myself, I was hoping the big moon wouldn't turn me back into the old Ledea. Looking at the clock, I did see it was midnight. Looking back out the window, something or rather someone caught my attention. A person was standing on the walking path that goes around the lake and staring up at Katherine's house. I didn't see him at first because he was so still—not moving at all. I kept staring. It was a man. With it being so dark, I couldn't tell if it was Star or not. I watched him as he walked down the dock and back and then headed down the path toward the little brown house.

I wouldn't have mentioned it to Katherine. In fact I kind of forgot about it until I over-heard Katherine and Will talking late one night. After watching a late movie in my own room, I came downstairs to get some juice when I overheard them.

"What can we do for Ledea? You know her better than I do, Katherine." Will was saying.

I was thinking maybe they didn't want me to live with them anymore. So I stood in the shadows and listened.

"I'm not sure what we can do. She has become my good friend, Will. She needs us. She's a lovely girl."

"I agree with you, Katherine. But, we've got a lot of bad stuff going on around the lake. What if she's involved?"

"There's no way Ledea is involved in any of this." Katherine said a little mad-like.

"We've had six robberies in the last several months, and although the cops say they don't have enough evidence yet, there's a lot of talk about the trouble coming from that little brown house on other side of the lake," Will went on like Katherine didn't know any of this.

"She's not a part of that, anymore, Will. There was trouble. That's why she moved out."

"Maybe she knows something. Maybe if she talked to the cops, we could stop all this." I was afraid Katherine and Will were going to fight. I had never heard them argue.

It was quiet for a while. Then, Katherine spoke. "I'm afraid for her, Will. Her husband, Stanley Johnson, he's not a decent man."

"Does Ledea need to move back in with her Mom?" Will asked.

"I think we can protect her better than her mom. As far as talking to the cops, I can ask her. I'm not sure Stanley even knows she's living with us. He may think she's back with her mom."

I forgot about the juice. Here was that stuff about Star being Stanley, again. How did Katherine know this? I went back upstairs and sat on the edge of the bed looking out on the lake. There he was again — the man — standing and looking at Katherine's house. I would have to tell them. This time, I ran down the stairs and burst into the living room where Katherine and Will were still sitting. A soft light lit a corner of the room. The rest was covered in darkness.

"There's a man. Outside. Looking up at your house. He's been here before. I don't know why." They both jumped; I was not the kind of girl to be bursting in on anything.

Will stood up right away. "A man? Who is it Ledea?"

"I don't know. I just thought with all the trouble going on around the lake that you might like to know."

Katherine gave me a quick hug as Will grabbed a flash light and went out the back door. She turned off the light in the corner, and both of us walked to the windows looking out onto the lake. He was still there. Standing with his hands on his hips like he couldn't make up his mind about something.

"Is Will going to be ok?" I asked.

"Let's watch. I think so." But I could tell Katherine was not sure. "I'm going to check on the children. You stay here and watch."

Will walked right up to the stranger and started talking to him. It was a short conversation. The stranger left and Will walked towards the house. I let him in the front door.

"Who is it? What does he want? Why is he here?" It all came out at once.

"Hold your horses, Ledea," Will answered. I thought Will surely had been talking to Star with words like *hold your horses*.

"I'm not sure who he was. Said his name was Junior, but he might have been lying. Who's to say. I'm not sure if I've seen this guy around before or not. Said he needed some night air and was out for a walk."

Junior? Why would Junior be staring at Katherine's house in the middle of the night? Junior had always been good to me. I could not say anything bad about Junior to Katherine or Will. I didn't know whether to return to my room or stand here with Will waiting to be questioned and not wanting to be—especially about Junior.

Katherine returned and asked Will, "Did you know him?"

"No. But I got a good look at him. I'd recognize him if he comes by again. Skinny guy with long, stringy hair. Seemed to be polite. But, it is a little strange."

"Let's get some sleep," Katherine said.

They followed me up the steps, but I heard Katherine whisper to Will. *You're sure it wasn't Stanley Johnson.* And Will answered, *"Yes, I'm sure."*

I was wishing it had been Stanley Johnson. Junior? Please no, I thought. Junior, I so wanted you to be good.

The weeks passed. Katherine and Will didn't bring up the subject of the robberies, the strange man outside their house, any of that. Katherine did take me to an eye doctor to have my eyes checked. He told me I needed a new prescription. The best part, besides being able to see better, was that I got to pick out these really cool frames. That same day, Katherine and I went back to the jewelry store where I had my ears pierced and we picked out new earrings. Some silver hoops and a pair of hearts with a little shiny diamond-like thing in the middle.

Will and Katherine also started to talk about a vacation to St. Thomas—a far away place with lots of beaches and islands and would I like to go—they wanted some help with the children. They showed me pictures from a travel magazine. The islands looked like chocolate mounds sticking out of a blue-blue sea. And, I wondered how people could live on them. Katherine said they would look flatter once we got there. Katherine also said that we needed to let Mel know about all this. I was an adult and could make my own decisions, but she said it was the considerate thing to do.

Lake Monster

When I was in school, ages ago, we read about the Loch Ness monster who lived in a lake by the same name in some country called Scotland. Those people who were unlucky enough to see it thought it might be about 30 feet long. Although scary to think about, I don't think this monster ever tried to kill anyone. The Lake Monster I'm talking about did.

So let's get on with the story. Just a reminder, Katherine and I were on our way to tell Mel about St. Thomas.

Sunday was always a good day to visit Mel, because we could all go to church. However, I have to admit that on this particular Sunday I wasn't thinking much about God's word. Instead, I had visions of islands, blue seas, and being on an airplane for the first time. Something, however, got my attention during church: the word *evil*. Pastor was talking about a king in the Old Testament who wondered how God, who is good, could use a wicked nation to bring punishment against God's own people, even though they were sinful. God's answer was *that evil, wherever it is found, always bears within it the seeds of its own destruction*. (The book of Habakkuk, if you want to check it out.) That word *evil* got my attention because even though I was living with Katherine's family, I knew Star was involved with evil and Star was my husband. A worry inside me grew. The words *evil, wherever it is found, seeds of destruction* settled in my brain and I could not get them out.

After church Katherine took us out to eat at the pizza place in town—Paradise Pizza is what they called it. Although it had a few palm trees, it was not paradise—not like the one I had been day dreaming about. Unfortunately, Pastor Simmons' words had filled my brain replacing the vacation day dream. So, when Katherine said, "Ledea, fill your mom in on our vacation plans."

"Uhmm?" was all I could say.

"Our vacation, remember?" Katherine looked at me puzzled; she knew how much this vacation meant to me.

"We're going to St. Thomas—I think." I kind of blurted.

"Where is this St. Thomas?" Mel asked while grabbing another piece of pizza. And with that I started to get excited again.

"Oh, Mel, it's the most beautiful place in the world. It's islands, sea, sky, fish…"

"Where is it, Ledea?" she asked again getting another napkin to wipe the pizza grease off her fingers. While I was eyeing Mel and wondering about her manners, Katherine took over.

"It's off the coast of Florida—a long ways. We'd like Ledea to go with us to help with the children. It will be quite an experience for her. She wanted to let you know." Katherine was looking at my mom carefully as if she needed her permission.

Mel took my hand and looked right into my eyes and said, "Ledea, that's wonderful. I'm happy for you."

Then she looked around the Paradise Pizza place like she was looking for something before she lowered her voice and said, "Besides, you need to get away. That husband of yours, Star, he's been looking for you."

"He's been here?" I asked and started looking around myself.

"No, silly. At the house," Mel answered in that still lowered voice. "A couple of times. With someone he calls Betsy."

"Betsy?" and before Mel could answer, "Did you tell him I'm living with Katherine?" Mel was making me nervous. Why hadn't she told me this sooner?

"Told him no such thing." Mel was shaking her head and kept shaking it as if she couldn't believe the mess we were in.

"Ledea will be safe with us." Katherine explained to Mel trying to make her feel better.

"What does he want?" I wondered out loud.

"Said you owed him some stuff. Money. Said you took stuff from the place you lived in with him." Mel told me.

"I took nothing! ... except my Bible and the radio Pastor Simmons gave me. We had nothing, Mel. How could I take anything?"

"He's a strange man, Ledea. I should have stopped you from marrying him. I just didn't know any better at the time." Mel had tears in her eyes and was still doing the head shaking thing like her head was set in motion and didn't know how to stop.

"We'll work this out, some how," Katherine said. "Maybe it's time we went to the police." I noticed how her hands were in a prayerful position, but her knuckles were white and we were not praying.

"Police?" I asked. "What would I tell them?" I was getting nervous—really nervous—so I folded my hands in a prayerful position. It was bad enough having Mel all shook-up and now, Katherine, too?

It was a quiet ride back to Katherine's home that day. Quiet because neither one of us were saying much. I guess we both had our own thoughts to sort out, but if our thoughts could be heard, there would have been a lot of noise.

At home that night, Katherine called the police with Will and me sitting around the table listening. The police explained that they had an eye on Stanley Johnson, the others, and the little brown house. They just needed more evidence before arrests were made. *Did we need protection? Did we feel safe?* Katherine asked Will. Will shrugged his shoulders. I shrugged mine. Katherine said it wouldn't hurt.

Everyone was *agitated,* Katherine's word, that night. It's like things were getting ready to blow up. Maybe right underneath our feet. I went down to the dock to clear my head. Katherine and Will were arguing about what to do. I had never heard them fight before. It bothered me; I felt like I was the reason. I sat at the end of the dock praying—not knowing what to ask for. There was a lot of *Dear God's* and deep sighs. That's probably why I didn't hear the monster behind me. Just like that—with no warning--someone pushed me into the water and came crashing in right after me—someone big and heavy pulling me down, down, down to the seaweed and slimy bottom of the lake. I tried to get away, but this person was much bigger and stronger pulling down on my skinny arms, ripping at my hair.

Pictures of Mel; Katherine; this place, St. Thomas, I'd never get to see because I was going to die kept floating around in my brain. I back-kicked with one of my legs and landed a good punch into a soft stomach and the grip on my arms loosened; but before I could flutter kick to the surface, a large, beefy hand grabbed my ankle. Good thing I'm skinny, because I just slipped through the fist, gave another kick and turned quick like to see a fat lady with blonde air circling her head in the dark waters. She was choking and I could see she was in trouble because someone else was in the water—grabbing *her* by the hair! With my lungs exploding and my heart attacking my insides, I struggled toward the surface when someone hands were on me, again. This time, pushing me up, up, up towards the dock ladder.

Breaking the surface of the lake, I gasped for air and could not get enough. Choking and feeling like a limp rag as I hung on to the ladder rung, I turned to face the person who had saved me—Junior. Just like that, he was gone again and within a few minutes had pulled the lake monster out of the water. *Betsy*! As he pulled her to shore, I spotted Katherine and Will running towards the lake. Will stopped to give Betsy the Red Cross breathing stuff, and Katherine ran to the end of the dock to check on me. We heard Betsy coughing up lake water and then start cussing—real bad words. Katherine left my side to call the cops.

Within minutes, they showed up—sirens and all—brought out the whole lake population with all that noise. You wouldn't believe the story Betsy told—me trying to drown myself and her trying to save me. Katherine said to me a couple of times, "Keep quiet, Ledea. The truth will come out." I looked around for Junior; he was gone. The cops left with Betsy in the back seat—soaking wet. Her hair still had seaweed in it and hung over one eye reminding me of the Loch Ness although, of course, there was no real comparison. She kept her eye on me the whole time she sat in the cop's car making me feel like the one who had done something wrong. Will and Katherine hugged me and both walked me up to my bedroom. If you can feel scared and safe at the same time—that would be it.

Star

I spent the next couple of weeks being kind of quiet. Mostly thinking how lucky I was to be alive, how lucky I was to have Katherine and Will in my life, what should I do about Star and Betsy, and where was Junior? Why did he seem to show up when I was in major trouble? How did he know and why did he care? As you can see, I had a lot to think about. I began to think that none of this would be straightened out until I broke all ties with Star. I had another worry. The vacation to St. Thomas was still possible. But, instead of excited, I was real worried about going to St. Thomas.

This is what I was thinking. Katherine, Will and their children, along with me, would be going to St. Thomas for a week. Some of the lake-side homes had been broken into and robbed while the people living there were vacationing. I was afraid for Katherine and Will. I was afraid Star was one of the robbers. I was married to Star. I had to do something about this. Somehow, I had ended up right in the middle of all of this. It made me sick to my stomach. I could not eat or sleep very well. *Agitated* was the word Katherine would use. I decided I must talk to Star. Even though it had ended so badly with him treating me like dirt, me finding a naked lady in our bed, and then discovering Betsy and Star on the beach making plans, I knew I had to talk to him face to face and finish all of this. Not to mention Betsy's part in all this. If she had drowned me, she would be a murderess. A murderess! Made me get goose bumps every time I thought of it and, believe me, I tried not to.

I would not visit Star at night. That was too scary, plus the thought of finding Betsy in my bed with Star still disgusted me. When Star was home, which had not been often, he usually slept late and left around 10:00 for his construction job. Yea, right, I thought "construction." Anyway, after breakfast and morning chores one day, Katherine asked me if I wanted to get groceries with her and the children. I told her I would just as soon watch a little TV—that one of my favorite game shows was on. She looked at me kind of funny. Katherine knew me pretty well. She was thinking, *Ledea, you've never watched a game show since I've known you.* But, get this, as smart as Katherine is, she shrugged her shoulders and said, "We'll be home in an hour or so. Enjoy your time, Ledea." And, they all left.

I heard the gravel crunch as the car left. Within seconds, I was out the front door and down the lake path to our little brown house. I hadn't walked this path in a long time. I hate to say it but my eyes and nose watered up, and I did a good job of feeling sorry for myself—thinking about what I thought I had and how it had turned out to be nothing—or worse than nothing—a huge mistake—evil, like Pastor Simmons said in his sermon. A couple of times, I thought about turning around and heading back. My palms were sweating and my heart was doing tiny flip-flops. I tried to stop it; it didn't work.

I went around to the front of the house. Star's pickup was there. I walked up to it and looked inside. Cigarette butts with lipstick on them, beads hanging from the rearview mirror, some kind of silly scarf besides Star's usual mess were inside. Was Betsy in jail or would I have to face them both? I opened the back door and stepped inside. There was Star sitting at the table eating scrambled eggs, toast and bacon. It was more food for breakfast than I had ever had in the little brown house. I looked around. No Betsy.

"L e d e a?" Star said my name in slow motion like he'd just been to the dentist or something and looked at me like he was trying to remember exactly who I was. His skin was pale under his dark whiskers. I wanted to ask him if he was sick, but I had business to take care of.

"Star?" I looked at him mad-like, not believing all that food he was eating when we had had nothing. He got this look of recognition on his face. Maybe my saying, "Star?" helped.

"Ledea, sit down. Hungry?" He kept chomping on the eggs leaving some of it on his whiskers.

Now, as you might expect, this was not what I expected. I did sit down—right across from him and looked at his food again.

"Where did that come from?" I asked.

"What?"

"That food. We never had any when I lived here."

"Oh. It's just eggs and bacon, Ledea. A man's gotta eat."

"Where's Betsy?" I changed the subject.

I saw a changed look in Star's eyes. He was thinking that Betsy was the reason I was there. It was not. But, I let him think that.

"Betsy? She isn't here. On the hot seat right now. Got herself in a bit of trouble. Heard it involved you, Ledea. Don't know what got into her."

"She's in jail?" I wanted to know.

"Jail. Her mom's. Not sure. She shouldn't done what she did, Ledea. Like I said, don't know what got into her."

154

"Where have you been?" Star changed the subject.

"Been?" Was Star really that out of it that he just thought I had been gone a few days and was returning?

"Yea, where you been? Got a check for us? Been working?"

Star's eyes were kind of funny, and I wondered if were drunk this early or if he had been smoking those sweet smelling cigarettes that always made him a little funny in the head. I didn't answer his question. I decided to get right to what we needed to talk about.

"Star. I know you've been robbing some of the lake shore homes. You and some other guys. It has to stop."

"Me? Ledea. You're going to have to take a backseat for a while until I get to the bottom of this. We might need to pack up and head to another state." Star was stronger than me, but his mind was messed up. He could not make me go with him anywhere.

"Star, you're an albastraws around my neck, and I will not go anywhere with you!" I wasn't sure where the *albastraws* came from—but it was stored in my brain somewhere and came out at the right time. Star looked at me surprised.

"You will not rob another home in this neighborhood or I will go straight to the police!" My voice kind of echoed around the little brown house.

I stood up quick-like and tipped the chair over— not meaning to; however, it was an accident, but a good one. When I turned at the door to take one last look, Star was rubbing his forehead with one of his hands mumbling, "…bull in a China shop, she is…"

I had this picture in my brain of Katherine's dishes, China, she called them, that she stored carefully in a hutch--Katherine's word. I had never been in a "China shop" before, but I could imagine it knowing about Katherine's dishes. Star and I had also watched this thing called running-with-the-bulls once when I was still living at Mel's. I think it happened in Spain. Anyway, these crazy people were letting bulls chase them down this street. Bulls in a China shop? Putting the two together, I finally understood one of Star's crazy lines he was so good at. Even though it took me a while, I had an answer for him.

"Bull in a china shop?" I asked Star and waited for him to raise his head and look right at me. His white face had taken on some red spots. "I can be that," I said letting Star get a good look into my eyes. Something he usually had not taken time to do.

I ran all the way home. Not so much afraid, but feeling kind of powerful. Bull in a China shop—yes, I could be that.

St. Thomas

If you're thinking that St. Thomas is someone in the same class as Pastor Simmons, you're wrong. St. Thomas is an island. You have to fly over Puerto Rico to get to it. We took a big plane to Puerto Rico, got off and waited for a smaller plane to come along to take us to St.

Thomas. From the air it looked too small for the plane to land, but as we got closer I could see it was going to work out. Once off the plane and in the airport, there were no windows or doors. Everything was wide open with people speaking different. When Katherine asked about our luggage, the man in uniform said, "we' en ga" instead of "We haven't got." I had to listen real close to understand anything. We finally got our luggage.

Katherine told me that St. Thomas was part of the Virgin Islands discovered by Columbus who named them after some lady and her 11,000 maidens. I felt like I was in another land, and I guess I was! After checking in at this huge place on the beach called the Wyndam, we looked out our window to see blue sky and these black mountains that looked like chocolate drops here and there in a deep blue sea. I didn't want to take my eyes off it. It was something out of a picture book. Katherine came up behind me and put her arm around my shoulders. "Amazing, isn't it?" I only shook my head. Any words wouldn't have worked.

Soon, Kyle and Kendra were begging to go swimming. We picked up snorkel equipment and headed for the beach where we swam with the fish. Right beside them, eyeball to eyeball—comfortable as could be. After swimming in the ocean, we swam in the pool. There were waterfalls and slides and palm trees surrounding the pool. After a couple of hours, Katherine and Will begged us to get out, and we all headed back to the room to dress for supper. Katherine said we had to call it *dinner* now.

We had to dress up a bit. We got in a taxi and after fifteen minutes or so of twisting and turning and honking—everyone seemed to honk to say "hi"—we ended up at the top of one of the tallest mountains on St. Thomas at a restaurant. Katherine said it was Mafolie's. She explained that we would be able to see the sea, the other islands and the town of Charlotte Amalie while we were eating. A soft breeze covered us as we ordered. I felt like I was on a cloud the whole time we ate.

We were at St. Thomas for a whole week. Swimming, snorkeling, visiting the shops and just relaxing took up our time. One day, the whole family rented a boat for a day-sail. The captain took us to different beaches to swim and snorkel. They even fed us. I got to ride up in front of the boat all the way back to our island with the wind whipping nicely at my hair and the sun browning my skinny self. The Lake Princess would have been proud.

The day we left, I was sad. I felt like a big part of Katherine's family. I had forgotten to even think about Star, Betsy, and the evil stuff happening around the lake. At St. Thomas, I could go to bed at night remembering everything I had done and seen. I would think about it over and over and store it in my mind like a treasure. When other people on vacation looked at our family, I imagined that they thought I was Katherine and Will's oldest daughter. I did a lot of *thank you, Gods* because of the warm family feelings and because of the most awesome sites I had ever seen.

The old feeling returned on the plane on the way home—a feeling of nervousness when I thought about Star, Betsy and some of Star's buddies. While the plane flew high above the cotton puffy clouds, I prayed that Katherine and Will's home would be in one piece—everything in order, like we left it.

Junior

We drove up to the Wilson Home around 8 p.m. All of us very tired after spending a week in St. Thomas. Although I was sitting in the back, I was peeking over Katherine and Will's shoulders as we got closer to their house—bug-eyed if anybody had looked at me—looking for clues of anything gone wrong. I was shaking as we carried our things inside. Katherine asked me if I felt ok.

"No. I mean, yes, I'm ok." I lied.

"You look like you're coming down with something, Ledea. Or, are you just tired?"

"Tired."

"Take your things upstairs, I'll fix a snack, and we'll all get some sleep."

I went from room to room downstairs, still carrying my suitcase. I still couldn't believe Katherine and Will's house was untouched.

"Ledea, what's wrong?" Katherine came up behind me.

"Nothing. I am hungry." I changed the subject quick and went back to the kitchen—relieved.

"I'll check the mail," Will yelled from the living room.

"I had it stopped. Remember?" Katherine yelled back. But Will was already out the door. He returned with a white square envelope in his hand. He turned it to show me. L E D E A was printed in big bold letters across the envelope.

"Got a secret admirer, Ledea?" he asked me with a wink.

"A what?" Now, I knew what he meant, but I was confused. Who would write me? Star's writing was scraggly—something you had a hard time reading.

"Here, open it." Will placed it in my hands.

I pulled a sheet of notebook paper out of the envelope. It read,

> *Dear Ledea,*
> *We need to talk. Trust me.*
> *Junior.*
> *PS... I will call you at Katherine's.*

"Well?" Will looked at me with his eyebrows up.

"Somebody wants to talk to me," I explained.

Now Katherine was getting a little worried. "Who?" she asked.

"I don't think you know him. He helped me the night I cut myself and had to have stitches. He helped me—that night—when I almost drowned. Junior was there."

Katherine looked at Will. Will's eyebrows went up and his eyes got bigger.

"Actually, Ledea, I do know Junior. I've known him a long time. His parents own several smaller cabins along the lake. He went to the same high school you did, but he spent most of his summers here." Katherine looked at Will as if she were trying to have him understand as much as me.

"You *know* him?" I couldn't believe Katherine would know someone like Junior. Although Junior had always been good to me—even kind and gentle—I thought he must have been part of Star's group, although not in the bad way most of the others were, since he showed up once in a while with them.

"Yes. I've known him ever since we've lived here. Some of the neighbors wondered about him—long hair, a loner, quiet—but I've never heard anyone say anything bad about him." Katherine explained.

"Oh." Was all I could say.

"Oh," was all Will could say.

"He wants to talk to you?" Katherine reminded all of us.

"Yes. You can read it." I handed the letter to Katherine and Will.

"He writes that he will call you. Are you all right with this, Ledea?" Will asked.

"With talking to him? It's ok, isn't it?"

Katherine looked at Will. Will looked at Katherine. They seemed to be studying each other's faces.

"I'm not sure." Katherine seemed to be thinking. "If you're ok with it, then, we'll be ok with it. But, I'd feel better if you met him here, at our house; you can talk on the porch. Are you ok with that? If he calls, that is."

I nodded my head. We all sat around the table that night eating toast with peanut butter and drinking milk—Kendra, Kyle, Will, Katherine, and me—all of us tired and full of memories. I wanted to remember St. Thomas forever, but Junior's letter kept interrupting what I wanted to keep in my head. Why did he want to talk to me?

Everyone was extra quiet that next day. We were either tired or waiting for the phone to ring. It finally rang after lunch. Katherine answered it.

"It's for you," she said, handing me the phone with a half smile.

"Hello?" My voice came out like it does first thing in the morning—when you haven't used it yet.

"Ledea, is that you? I can barely hear you?" Junior asked me. His voice was soft, too.

"It's me. I got your note."

"Good. Hi."

"Hi."

"Can I come over or do you want to meet me somewhere?"

"Hmmm—can you come over to Katherine's house? We can talk on the porch. Katherine said it would be ok."

"You told them about my note?" Junior asked. He didn't ask like it was a bad thing; he just asked liked he was wondering.

"It was in their mailbox."

"Oh, yea, guess it was." Silence.

"So, you're coming over?"

"Sure. When would be a good time?" He asked—polite like.

I covered up the phone and turned to Katherine, "When?" I asked her.

Katherine shrugged her shoulders and whispered, "It's up to you."

"You could come over now or after supper."

"Ok…." Junior seemed to be thinking. "I'll be there around 7."

"I'll meet you on the porch."

"Thank you, Ledea."

"Good bye."

"Good bye."

As soon as I got off the phone, I was wishing I had told Junior to come over right away. I couldn't stand the suspense. Every minute seemed like ten. Did he want to talk to me about Star? So far, Junior had been kind of mysterious—you know, like in and out of my life at weird times. I didn't admit this to you before, because I'm supposed to be a *married woman*. But after Junior held me on the beach and took me to the emergency room, I had this warm cuddly feeling whenever I thought about him. I wanted to think about him a lot, but I always tried to stop myself—thinking it not right.

I only ate half my supper. Katherine had made a pot roast and this yummy chocolate brownie pudding. My stomach was too nervous. I helped her clear the table, went upstairs to brush my hair and put on a little lip gloss As I was coming downstairs, the porch doorbell rung.

"Ledea, it's for you?" Kendra yelled.

Katherine held the front porch door for me as I walked out onto the porch with Junior watching me like I was Miss America or someone really special. I guess he didn't know what to do or say with Katherine sticking around.

I offered Junior a chair, and Katherine left. I sat on the porch swing, but not for long. The squeaking was like scraping fingernails on a chalkboard, so I switched to a rocking chair. Junior kept watching me the whole time. Those dark eyes that at first scared me a little—not knowing if he met bad or good—now, I wanted to get lost inside them. I was relieved when some words finally came to him.

"Ledea," Junior put his forearms on his knees and leaned towards me. "I don't know where to start."

I didn't know what to say. It was Junior that wanted to come, so I just put my forearms on my knees and looked at him. It was that way—our faces were about two feet apart.

"My parents, they own some lake property. That's why I'm here a lot. I look after it. The little brown house you lived in with Star, that's one of them."

"Oh." I was starting to wonder if Junior wanted money from me—for rent or something.

"You probably thought that I was one of Star's buddies. It might have looked like that, but I'm not. I wanted you to know that." Junior was licking his lips a lot like he was nervous. I had not seen him like this.

"OK." I said softly still wondering what he wanted. He looked around to see if anyone else was listening and then put his arms back on his knees. I sat up—my elbows were getting sore.

"I want you to be safe." He took a deep breath. "Star is not good for you or for anyone else."

"I've been staying at Katherine's. They said I could. They want me to be safe, too."

"This is a good place for you. I think you should stay. Don't go back to the little brown house. Things are going to get worse, Ledea. Don't go back." He sat there shaking his head.

"I won't. I got what I needed."

"Good." He just kept staring at me, and I wondered if he was out of stuff to say and didn't know how to leave. So, I stood up trying to make it easy for him. He took my hand and pulled me back to the chair.

"Ledea, you don't remember me do you?"

"Remember you? Of course, I do. You took me to the emergency room, you saved my life when Betsy attacked me, you held…." And, then, I stopped because I was starting to blush. He smiled. He turned a little pink, too.

"I was in high school with you, Ledea." …. a little memory of what Katherine had said earlier about Junior being in high school with me crept in; but I had let it get past me.

"You what?"

"High school. I was there—with you." He took a deep breath. "I was also in the car with you the night of the accident."

"What?" He nodded his head. "Why?" I asked.

"You mean *why was I there?*"

I shook my head slowly trying to remember that night so many years ago. The night Maria and I made a poor decision, and she died.

"I used to hang out with some of those guys. I was athletic, but not smart or rich, that kind of thing. So, sometimes, it worked for me to hang out with them. There were a lot of guys in the car. It was dark. You wouldn't have noticed me, anyway."

I sat shaking my head. I couldn't believe it. My face got hot and my eyes watered.

"Don't be mad at me. It wasn't my idea. I told them not to bother you and Maria. I'm sorry."

"Is that what you came to tell me?" I asked.

"I want you to stay away from Star. I want you to be safe. I care about you." Junior was wiping his hands on his jeans—nervous like. "I always have."

"What?" Now, I was really confused.

"I knew where you lived when you were in town with your mom. I never had enough nerve to come to your house and you didn't have a phone."

"No. We didn't."

"Then, after the accident, I didn't want to talk to you thinking you would hold it against me—me being one of them."

"Gosh. That was so long ago."

"Yea, it was. I just wanted you to know." Junior replied so quiet it was almost a whisper.

"All right..." I wanted to make Junior feel better about all of this, but I could think of nothing else to say.

"I should go."

Not wanting him to leave feeling worse than me, I took his hand. I wanted him to hold me like that night after Star's big party. I didn't want him to go.

"I'm not mad at you. About the accident, that is. Maria and I shouldn't have gone. It was a bad night. For all of us." I so wanted to make him feel better.

"Yea. A lot has happened since then."

"A lot. I really don't know how it's all going to turn out," I said taking his other hand so that I held them both. "I'm really lucky to have Katherine's place to live and a job besides." Junior kept looking at me—he didn't know what to say now. "I'm also lucky to have Katherine as a friend."

"I'd like to be a friend, too." Junior said this as his eyes took on that mysterious almost-dark look.

"You are—my friend." I squeezed both of his hands, and Junior squeezed back.

"I'd like that." He squeezed my hand again and walked out the squeaky, front porch door. He turned to wave and then ran down the lake path in the direction of the little brown house.

James

I couldn't go to sleep that night—of course. Thinking about Junior and thinking I shouldn't be thinking about Junior. Worried still about Star and Betsy and the gang they hung out with in the little brown house that used to be mine and Star's. My brain was bouncing around like a ping-pong ball—back and forth— from this to that until it was driving me nutty. So, I tried to think about Mel, Pastor Simmons, Ms. Stenzel, and even Maria. I thought about what Junior had said about knowing me in high school. I thought and thought and thought about him being in school with me and could not come up with a single memory of Junior. I always thought I had not fit in; maybe, Junior had felt the same way—no one really knowing or caring about him. I so wish I had known him, then. If I had, maybe I wouldn't have married Star and maybe I wouldn't be in the mess I was in now.

The whole memory of high school made my head hurt even more. What else had *I* missed? Should I ask Katherine for an aspirin? Wanting to calm myself, I concentrated on Pastor Simmons. Remembering some of the things he had said to me like, *The secret is Christ in me*.....and, then, I remembered Pastor Simmons saying to me, more recently, *Ledea, read James*. Even though we were studying James in our Bible study group, we had not met lately. James was a short chapter. I threw the covers off, turned on the bedside lamp, got out my Bible and turned to James in the New Testament.

I re-read the stuff about counting it all joy when you meet various trials because it gives you the steadfastness. And if someone doesn't have wisdom, you should ask God for it. Then in Chapter 3, James talked about wisdom again when he wrote in verse 17, *But the wisdom from above is first pure, then peaceable, gentle, open to reason, full of mercy and good fruits...* And, of course, I thought of Katherine. But I also thought of someone new: Junior! Junior was peaceable, gentle, open to reason. Did Junior know the secret? And, then, I thought about myself thinking I should try to be better at all of these things.

I placed the Bible on my bed stand with the idea that I would read and re-read James until I understood it better. I don't remember falling asleep, but I know I did because of what comes next.

Destruction

A loud noise awoke me. So loud it made me jump out of bed and on my feet without even thinking about it. The clock said 2 a.m. Was it a gun? Was someone in Katherine and Will's house? I stepped to the window facing the lake. That's when I saw it. Flames. Huge, shooting flames coming from the little brown house. Even in the night, I could see the black smoke becoming a part of the clouds. Crackling sounds and popping noises soon followed.

In the dark of night, I ran like a wild woman down two flights of stairs and burst into Katherine and Will's bedroom to tell them. Will called the fire department. They were already on the way. Out on the front porch, all of us heard the sirens and watched from a distance as the flames started to die.

"Ledea, are you ok?" Katherine asked me.

"My house," was all I could say. Although it was not mine and had not been for some time.

Katherine sat beside me on the front steps. The wind carried the heat and the smell from the fire.

"Do you suppose Star was there?" I asked not even looking at Katherine and not wanting to know.

"We have no way of knowing." She pulled me close to her and stroked my hair.

There was no more sleeping that night for Will, Katherine, and me. Around 5 o'clock, Katherine pulled some bacon and eggs out of the refrigerator and pancake mix off the cupboard shelf and put us all to work.

"We need to stay busy," she said. And with that she handed me the eggs, Will the bacon, and she started mixing up pancakes. It was surprising how hungry we were. We ate without conversation; it's like we had an understanding that things were going to change but didn't even know how to talk about it.

I wanted to go look at what was left of the little brown house. Katherine told me we probably wouldn't be able to get close—that they would have it roped off. The fire story made the front page in the Lakeside News that came in the afternoon.

Lakeside fire claims lives.   It's what the newspaper said.   And, I started imagining Star dead; I didn't mean to.   This vision of Star burning with Betsy was in my head and wouldn't go away.   I didn't know how to feel about any of this.   Star was my husband, but his new girlfriend, Betsy had tried to kill me.   Star's idea?   Betsy's?   Would I ever know.   If they were both ok, would I be relieved?

There was a picture of three firemen spraying down the outside of the house.   Under the picture, it read, "Members of the fire department stayed at the scene of a fatal house fire throughout the morning."   Katherine read the article to me because I was too agitated to read it on my own.

Deputy State Fire Marshal David Snider hopes to have more information later today about what caused a fatal house fire…The blaze claimed several lives. Names will be released after family members are informed….. Without thinking, I looked at the door expecting someone to knock.   The article said "several lives." Betsy?

And, then I thought of someone else: *Junior?* Where was he? Was he with them? And I became sick-agitated at the thought. Laying my head on my forearms at the kitchen table, I tried to make the sick feeling go away. I would not be able to think or get anything done feeling this way. That's when the back door-bell rang. Katherine rubbed my back as she passed.

"Hello officer," Katherine stated quietly.

"Hi, Mrs. Wilson.   Sorry to bother you." Everything was quiet for a few seconds. "I understand

Stanley Johnson's wife lives with you. Is that correct?" I could feel their eyes on my back.

"Yes, Ledea lives with us. Can I take a message?"

"It would be better if I spoke to her. Is she here?" I guess he didn't recognize my backside. I wanted to disappear.

"Yes, Ledea's here. Please come in. Can I get you a cup of coffee?"

I heard the kitchen chairs scratching the floor as they were being pulled out.

"Mrs. Johnson, I'm Officer Makstead. I've been sent to inform you that we are unsure of your husband's whereabouts."

I lifted my head to see a man in uniform—old enough to be my father. He looked tired and worn-out himself.

"You mean Star's not dead?" I asked him.

"We're not sure." Officer Makstead looked at Katherine as if she could help.

"The bodies were badly burned. There were several. We have not been able to identify everyone yet. We just thought we should let you know that at this point we are not sure of anything."

"Several? Who?" I thought of Junior.

"We're not sure." He looked at Katherine, again. "When we have more news, we will get a hold of you." With that, he stood and told Katherine he would let himself out. I heard the screen door slap shut. I stood up quickly.

"Katherine, I have to go."

"Go? Where, Ledea?" She asked.

"The little brown house. I have to see it. I used to live there with Star."

Why did I have to explain this to Katherine?

"I'm not sure Ledea," Katherine was unsure. I was not. I ran through the house, out the front door and headed toward the lake path. I could hear Katherine behind me.

"I'll go with you, Ledea. Slow up. Please wait."

I couldn't slow down. My whole body was pumped up. I had to see it. I could smell it long before we arrived—a strong smoke smell. And the smell of death. I had never smelled anything like it before, but a person knows it for what it is. Katherine finally caught up and stood beside me as we looked at the little brown house—surrounded by yellow ribbon. A charred outer shell with broken windows hid what was inside. A couple of firemen watched a few smoky spots.

"It's gone, all of it," I whispered to Katherine.

Katherine only shook her head. "Let's go home, Ledea."

"How did it start? Who did this?" I wanted to know.

"I don't know, Ledea. But, I'm sure they will have answers soon."

Katherine and I walked home. She held me by the wrist, not tight-like, but in a way so that I could not escape. Even though I felt like it. It had been a horrible thing to see and I cried all the way. Kendra and Kyle met us at the door with ...*Ledea, are you all right? Ledea, do you want to play a game with us? How about a snack?...* trying to get me to feel better.

I went up to my room and pulled the shade looking out onto the lake and the little brown house, but I was restless. Katherine called up to me about doing some errands and grabbing lunch. I washed my face and headed downstairs. Katherine had a good idea; it just didn't turn out that way. Everywhere we went, people seemed to be whispering about me. *That's her. The girl from the little brown house. You know, Stanley Johnson's wife. Wonder why she wasn't there. Living with the Wilson's I hear.* Some people who usually spoke to Katherine avoided us by turning their grocery carts and heading another direction. When we ate, no one seemed to want to be near us. I felt guilty and yet could not put my finger on one thing I had done wrong. Except, I was Star's wife. I so wished I was not.

When we got home, I asked Katherine why everyone seemed to be talking about me.

"A lot has been happening around the lake during the last few months, Ledea, and now this. People aren't sure what to believe. In a few weeks or months, the answers will come out, and they will have someone else to talk about. Try not to let it bother you."

"It makes me feel like I've done something wrong. Could I have stopped any of this?" I asked her.

"You have done nothing wrong. And, I honestly don't know how you could have stopped this. Stanley Johnson is not a good man. You did fall in love with him, Ledea, so you must have seen something in him. I

174

don't know why some things happen." She sighed and then smiled—just a bit. "But I do know that if we have God in our hearts, it all will work out—maybe not the way we planned it, but he does love and care for us in an unbelievable way. We can trust him that it will all work out."

"I need to leave," I kind of blurted out.

"Leave?" Katherine stopped smiling.

"I need to go back to live with Mel. It's not fair to you and Will and Kyle and Kendra to have me here. People are talking about me. It would be best if I weren't here."

"Ledea!" was all she said.

"You have all been a family to me, but I need to be gone for a while." I felt really sad saying this, but I felt it was the right thing to do. Katherine was chewing on her lower lip; something I had never seen her do before. She started to say something and then stopped.

"If that's what you want to do…." She didn't know what else to say.

"Yes, I'll go pack," and I walked up the stairs not fast like I used to take the steps two at a time, but slow because my heart was so heavy that it made my legs heavy, too. I heard Katherine's voice say "Ledea" a few times as she walked toward the bottom of the steps, but she never came up to my room.

Mel

I wanted to cry when I carried my stuff up the walk to Mel's house. I had forgotten how awful it was—needing paint, weeds for a yard, the door hanging crooked on its hinges. Mel even looked older to me. Did she know? Had she heard about the fire on the news or read about it in the paper? Katherine helped me with the few things I had packed. As she hugged me, I saw Kendra and Kyle staring out the car window—their faces pressed next to the glass. I didn't know if they were sad to have to leave me or if they were sad because Mel's house was such a sorry site.

As I waved from the door, I heard Kyle ask his mother, "Does Ledea have to stay there?" Like it was a punishment for me. It made me feel bad twice—once because it was Mel's house and Mel was my mother. The second time I felt bad because I would miss the Wilson house, the comfort, the good food. And then I felt guilty-bad, because Mel had never had any of this.

Mel gave me a hug and helped me carry my things to my old room. It hadn't changed a bit. Same thread-bear tan bedspread, same faded rug on the floor, same shade pulled down over the window. I looked in the mirror over the dresser and saw someone who no longer fit in. With my new glasses, new hairstyle, pierced ears and clothes Katherine had bought for me, I felt out of place in my mother's house.

"Ledea?" Mel stood in my doorway looking at me.

"Yes, Mom." I answered

"You're different. So beautiful." And she just stood there like she didn't know who I really was.

"It's me, Mom. Guess I look a little different." And then I said, "Sorry, Mel," not knowing why.

"Sorry?"

"Yea, I'm sorry I didn't let you know I was coming. I hope it's ok."

"Ledea, you can always come back." She gave a quick pat to the doorway as if to let me know she really meant what she said. Kind of like a judge slapping his gavel.

"Thanks, Mom. I'm not sure how long I'll be here. Do you think the Red Owl would take me back?"

"Star? Where is he?" Mel changed the subject.

"I'm not sure. A lot has happened."

She turned and I followed her into the kitchen. From the backside, Mel looked older. Her shoulders and back were hunched and I thought of her as an old woman. She put the tea kettle on, got out some packets of hot chocolate and two mugs. As I sat at the table and waited for the whistle of the pot, a memory came. Star and I eating fishsticks after I prayed, "Come Lord Jesus be our guests." I wanted to hate him for all he had done—to me and to others. But, then I pictured him at Red Owl ordering dark chicken, mashed potatoes and gravy—lots of it. In this picture was a young girl, Ledea. I took a deep breath realizing how I *had* changed. Knowing Star, knowing Katherine, knowing Junior had changed me. I can't say I felt bad; I can't say I felt good. It was kind of a life thing. Some good things had happened; some bad things had happened. It's just the way it was.

"So, you really don't know where Star is?" Mel asked as she poured the steaming, hot water into our mugs.

"Mom, there was a bad fire. Our little brown house, where Star and I used to live, is gone. Totally gone. Some people died. There's lots of talk. Star could have been in the house. But, he was gone a lot. So, I'm not sure. They said they'd let me know."

"Oh, Ledea..." was all she said.

"Yea, it's not a good thing. That's why I came home. People are talking. I thought it best to be away from it all."

"Oh, Ledea..." Her head started doing this head shaking thing it is so good at. I wanted to take her head and hold it still.

Mel felt so bad for me. The marriage. Me coming home. Me looking for work. She didn't know what to say. I tried to change the subject.

"How are Grandma and Grandpa?" I sipped my hot chocolate and burned my tongue.

"Who?"

"Your parents? How are they?" You may remember that Mel and I never spent much time with her parents. Mel's choice. But, she never really spoke poorly of them either.

"That's another story." Mel poured more hot water into her cup. I didn't see how she could drink it when it was so hot.

"What's wrong? Are they ok?"

"Just last week, my sister from San Antonio drove all the way here to move them into the assistive living home at the edge of town. You would have thought they would have asked me, but I guess with no car or anything, I couldn't have moved them anyway."

"Why? What's wrong? What's going to happen to their house?"

"Poor health, Ledea. It happens."

"I'm sorry, Mel. Did you get to visit with your sister?"

"Oh, Mary took us all out to lunch on the day she left. Talked about her two sons, one an attorney, one in banking or something to do with money. Couldn't understand a lot of it. She's always lived in a different world than you and me, Ledea. We don't have a lot in common."

Not having any sisters or brothers I could not imagine how Mel might feel about this.

"Their house, that's another topic," she went on. Mel gave me a look I couldn't quite figure out.

"Their house? Why? What's wrong with it?"

"Nothing that I know of." Mel acted like she was scared of what she was about to say next. "Mary said I might as well move in and take care of it. Somebody needed to. None of the family wants it sitting empty. I guess she's the family spokesman or something like that." Mel kept looking at me. It's a good thing I came home. This was a lot for Mel to sort out.

"What about this house? You've always lived here." I looked around not liking what I saw.

"My folks bought this for me before you were born. It's not much, but it has always been home to me."

"If you decide to move, when would you go?" I asked thinking the move for Mel would be a little like me moving into live with Katherine. Grandpa and Grandma's house was old but it had been taken care of. There was a porch on the front with a swing, two stories, and beautiful furniture.

"Whenever I'm ready. I have the keys. To the house," she said almost like she was bored. I expected more of a reaction from my mom.

"Wow, Mel. Are you excited?"

"Lived here most of my life. Lived here not even feeling real welcomed in my folks' own house—the place where I grew up. I don't know. Should I be?"

I didn't know what to say to her. Although Mel was my mom, it hit me that there was a lot I didn't know about her and how she felt about things. We didn't have those kind of conversations when I was growing up. It was more like, *did you get enough to eat, are you warm enough, turn down that TV* conversations. We didn't seem to ever talk about anything that others would call deep.

Mel was talking to me more than she ever had before. I guess we had some catching up to do. The next day Mel brought empty boxes home from work. This was a sign to me. We packed a few things, and I walked to the Red Owl to ask for a job application being surprised how friendly everyone was. I didn't know if they knew about the fire or not. Before I left the store, the manager called out to me.

"Ledea, you can start next Monday?" He asked while stuffing someone's groceries in plastic bags.

"Start? What time?" I wasn't used to yelling and felt everyone must have been looking at me.

"The usual. You remember?"

I walked closer to him. "8 a.m. Right?"

"See you then." He winked. I left feeling happy.

Later that day, Mel and I walked to Grandma and Grandpa's house. We walked up the porch steps, and Mel carefully put the key in the key hole to the main door. With a click, Mel turned the doorknob and we stepped in. How long had it been? A Christmas long ago? I must have been in junior high. The memory of it started rushing back. A full house. Aunts, uncles, cousins—strangers all of them. Lots of smiles in the house, but still feeling out of place. I kept asking Mel when we could go home—to *our* house. After a huge meal with more food than I had ever seen at one time, we were supposed to open gifts. I had a stomach ache—I had eaten too much and still wanted to go home.

"What are you thinking, Ledea?" Mel asked me.

"Christmas. It's the last time we were here. How old was I?"

"Thirteen, maybe fourteen. It was the last time we were both here. Sad, isn't it—to think that my parents lived within walking distance of my house and I never visited them."

"Why? Why was that?' I asked Mel as we both stood in the entryway trying to take it all in and remember things from the past.

"Well, there was a big argument that Christmas—an argument about how I was not raising you right. Everyone had an opinion—talking about us as if we weren't even there. After Christmas dinner, I took you into this very entryway, pulled our worn-out coats out of the closet, and we walked home."

I noticed that Mel was crying. I wanted to comfort her but didn't know how.

"It was awful cold. I felt bad that you had no mittens. We sat in front of the stove when we got home to warm up. Next day, who turns up? My parents and sisters with their gifts for us that we hadn't opened. When I saw them walking up our walk, I locked the door. You and me went to the back bedroom—maybe, you didn't even know. Haven't seen any of them since—except for Mary who came to move Mom and Dad. My parents used to drop by; they kind of stopped, too. Don't know what I did."

"I'm sorry, Mel." It was all I could say. I thought of how important family was to the Wilson's and realized how Mel and I had missed out on a lot. Maybe it couldn't be helped.

"I did the best I could, Ledea. Never married. He was a bum. Wouldn't have been a good father. Didn't want to be a father at all."

"Mom?" Mel was starting to talk on and on. I was getting a little worried. It wasn't like her to do this. "It's ok. You were a good mom. I never had any complaints."

Mel wiped her tears away with her sweatshirt sleeve, made a funny noise with her nose and said, "Well, might as well look around and decide if we want to move or not."

Mel didn't talk about any of this anymore, but she did more packing the next day and told me to bring any extra boxes home from the Red Owl if they had them. We needed them to pack our things. Some of our stuff we just set out on the curb hoping the garbage men would pick it up. Later, I saw some of our neighbors picking through it; maybe, it was a tad bit better than some of the stuff they had. You see, Grandma and Grandpa's house was already full of everything we needed to live. The kitchen had pots and pans and dishes like I had never seen before. The bedrooms were full of plushy pillows and quilts. Every room had more than enough furniture.

One day before moving, I walked around our old neighborhood. Maria's parents still lived in the same house. The dogs were different but still barking and mean looking. Some boys were working on an old pickup parked right in the front lawn—cussing and throwing things. I hurried on. Cracks in sidewalks, loud music, shades pulled, peeling paint, rusted out cars, broken toys. Did brokenness go along with being poor— not having enough? Some people seemed to have more than enough; some not enough of anything. I would not miss this neighborhood, but I *wanted* to miss it. It had been my growing-up life. It was a part of who I was—I wanted to keep it because it was a part of me. And, then, I thought of something—if Junior was still alive, would he be able to find me? *If Star were still alive, would he be able to find me?* Both thoughts scared me in different ways.

Cinderella

That's who I felt like—Cinderella. Mel and I lived in a house with a front porch with a swing. My bedroom had cushiony lavender carpet with flowered wall paper. The quilt on the bed was lumpy soft; the pillows puffy big. Mom gave me Grandma and Grandpa's room, the big one, because she wanted the bedroom that faced the street saying she liked checking out what was going on in the street below from a *second story* window. Something she was not used to. My room had a corner bookshelf with an encyclopedia set and knick-knacks—I guess that's what they called them. Glass figures of angels and animals that sparkled when the morning sun came in. And—you won't believe this—my own bathroom. The tub was big with claws for feet. There was a makeup mirror with a special light. Grandma's bubble bath and lotions sat in a basket beside the tub.

Besides Mel's and my bedroom, there was another one that Grandpa and Grandma used for storage. It was piled high with boxes. You could walk around in there if you like getting lost. That's how full it was. Also, upstairs, at the top of the steps, there was a large hallway, as big as a room, just for sitting and doing nothing. There was a small couch—Mom said it was a loveseat—I wondered about that one. Also a chair big enough for two had a footstool in front of it with a lamp and stand beside it. Mel said we could read books there if we wanted peace and quiet. I got out the S encyclopedia and placed it on the lamp stand for later— wanting to know more about St. Thomas and to help me remember those things I did not want to forget about what happened during my vacation with Katherine's family.

That's just the upstairs. Downstairs was good, too. A large living room had two matching couches, lamps, a TV, a bookshelf full of Reader's Digest condensed books, and a coffee table with Grandma's last Ladies Home Journal. If you walked under a large arch, you were in the dining room with a big wooden table with six chairs arranged around it. A cupboard with glasses and dishes was at one end, kind of like Katherine's China hutch, and a large picture window looked out at the neighbor's flower garden. If you walked under another archway, you would be in the kitchen—my favorite room downstairs. Grandma's kitchen was almost as big as our entire old house. Another table with four chairs was in the backside of the kitchen close to a big window that looked out into the back yard. Grandpa had hung bird feeders and waterers. Sometimes, there were yellow, red and blue birds hanging out there—just for us to watch. I would have to get out the B encyclopedia and learn the birds' names. More about the kitchen: cupboards lined two whole sides and there was an island (Mel's word) in the middle for a workspace. I would definitely have to learn to cook with a place like this. On the opposite side of the wall where the table was, there was a washer and dryer next to a door that led into the basement.

Mom and I checked out the basement together. It was mostly empty except for the necessary things, like the furnace, water softener, several shelves of empty canning jars, and a de-humidifier to keep it all dry. Mel and I did a little dance after checking it all out like *we can't believe we get to live here.* It was good for both of us to act silly.

After several telephone conversations with Mel's sister, Mary, we found out we could use the car and we were to sell our old house. The money from that would help us with some of the cost of keeping up Grandma and Grandpa's house. The car was parked inside the garage in the backyard. We walked out there together.

"You get the door, Ledea. I'll follow you." Mel was acting like a scaredy cat—like she'd never seen a real car before.

"No. You go, Mel. It's your parent's car." With that I pushed her forward.

Mel and I both got in the car. She sat behind the wheel because I made her. Neither of us had a license to drive. Mel put her hands on the steering wheel and acted like she was driving. I had never seen Mel like this. We laughed until tears were running down our cheeks and we were worn out.   It's what some people call a belly laugh and it was good for both of us.

We tried to visit Grandma and Grandpa once a week just to fill them in on how things were going *back home* as they called it.   Grandpa was often playing cribbage when we came, and Grandma always had a new craft to show us.

"Not worth much," she would always say, "But, gotta have something to do."

"It's nice," Mel would always say.

"Do you think so?" Grandma would ask.   Same conversation every time.

We even ate with them a couple of times. Grandma and Grandpa would introduce us to other people in the home saying "daughter" and "grand daughter" like we had always been part of the family. I wondered about that. All those years that passed with us hardly ever seeing them. But, whenever Mary called, she said we were doing a good job of taking care of everything, and I guess Mel felt more a part of her family than she ever had.

I started back to work with my new look—thanks to Katherine.   And, my new house—thanks to Mel's family—feeling like Cinderella. Without the prince.

The Lake Princess

Several weeks passed.   Mel and I were eating hamburger-helper one night with a shredded lettuce salad—all from the Red Owl grocery shelves, of course, when the phone rang. We both jumped—we still weren't used to the phone ringing. I looked at Mel and Mel looked at me. It kept ringing. After four rings, I got up and answered it. It was Katherine. Hearing her voice made me feel funny—I had these two separate families I felt a part of. Guess I was lucky. She wanted me to visit. "Stay the whole weekend," Katherine said. "We'll have lots of fun. Kendra and Kyle can't wait to see you."

When I asked Mel if it was ok to go, she just waved her hand at me. The kind of wave that says *get out of here; why are you even askin'*....

I packed a small bag, and Katherine picked me up after work on Friday afternoon. We hugged before getting into the car. All the way to the lake, Kendra and Kyle were saying things like, *Ledea, do you know... Ledea, remember when... Ledea, we saved your room.... Ledea, when are you coming back to stay?* On and on, so many questions; I couldn't answer them all. We prayed that night before our meal. Katherine and Will always made the sign of the cross after the prayer and then had a quick kiss. I watched them. I have to tell you my heart ached. I don't honestly know if it was because I missed them or because I wanted love—the kind of love like they had for each other.

We played Monopoly; Will won. Kendra and Kyle walked me upstairs to my old room. Kyle carried my bag, and Kendra chatted about some new friends she had made. They left with a "See you in the morning, Ledea. We're having waffles, your favorite, right?"

"Right," I answered and hugged them a good night. I sat on the bed. My window facing the lake still had its shade pulled. I wanted to look. I really *wanted* to go down to the lake. The clock said 10:15—too late to be out. Katherine would be upset if I did. So, I slipped into my PJs, climbed into bed and folded my hands in prayer. "Thank you, God," was all that came to mind before falling to sleep.

When I awoke, the clock said 5 a.m. I lifted the shade. Still dark outside, but the moon lit up part of the lake and the Wilson's dock. Someone was sitting on the bench facing the water at the end of the dock. Wide awake, I slipped on yesterday's clothes. Katherine? Will? Quietly leaving the house and walking across the wet grass with bare feet, I reached the dock. The person was so still that for a while I wondered if it was a person or merely a shape that looked like a person. I turned toward the house; should I go back? Softly, a step at a time, I walked to the end of the dock. A person with long, dark curly hair sat with his back facing me. I *knew* who it was. Was he asleep? My heart skipped a whole bunch of beats and then raced forward. Stepping closer, I saw him—his face—eyes closed, in a deep sleep. In his hand, he held a pheasant feather: brown with black stripes.

Sitting beside him, I lightly tapped his hand with my pointer finger. He didn't move, so I giggled—how could he be so out of it. Tapping him again, Junior jumped a little, and then a lot, seeing it was me.

"Ledea!" He rubbed his eyes and coughed a little.

"Junior!" I couldn't believe it was him. No names had been released from the fire thing. My smile covered my whole face.

"Ledea?" He asked like he couldn't believe it either.

"Junior?"

"Where did you come from?" he asked.

"I'm visiting Katherine."

"Oh. Wow. I didn't expect to see you so soon."

"I didn't expect to see you at all. I mean…"

"No, its ok. I understand. The fire. Maybe, you thought…."

"Yea, I did. But, I hoped you were ok."

I really wanted to take Junior in my arms and squeeze the day-lights out of him I was so thankful he was alive and ok. But, of course, I couldn't. I was too shy, and I *was* married.

"I was gone when it all happened. At my folks'. They thought it best for me to stay away until everything settled down." Junior kept staring at me. He was good at that.

"What are you doing here?" I changed the subject.

"Here? Oh, you mean on the Wilson dock?" I nodded. "Well, here, this is for you." And, he opened my palm with his one hand and put the feather in it with the other one. And, then, just held it. "For you," he repeated.

"For me?" I couldn't take my eyes off his eyes. But I wanted to look at the feather, too. My Lake Princess feather!

"I remember the story you told me about the Lake Princess. I loved you for that," he explained.

"You what?" Junior had said the word *loved*. My heart was doing fluttery things and I felt like marshmellows inside.

"I liked the idea about you being the Lake Princess. It said a lot about you. About what you liked and. . . who you are."

"Oh." I should have looked down at the feather. After all that is what we were talking about. But, my eyes were attached to Junior's and I couldn't even make them look at this feather he had gotten just for me.

"Anyway, I got it for you." He took his hand away and his eyes away from mine and stared out at the lake. We both did. I broke the silence.

"Thank you, Junior," I said turning to get a good look at him again.

"You're welcome," and he turned and looked into my eyes with that intense look.

I knew all this staring stuff had to stop, so I brought up you-know-who.

"Do you know where Star is?"

"No. I'm not sure, but I don't think he was in the cabin that night. The rumors are that it was a group from out of state—come to pick up drugs—Star not being home—and then sticking around waiting for him when the whole thing blew up during the middle of the night."

"Gosh. That's terrible."

"Yea. They're just starting to put the facts together and sort it all out. I'd say they're on the look-out for Star.

He's got a reputation around here, and not a good one." He looked at me after saying that. "I'm sorry, Ledea. I didn't mean...."

"You don't have to apologize. I guess, after a while, I figured out that Star was up to no good."

"That's why I'm here. You really have to be careful, Ledea. You can't trust him. I'm not sure what he'll do next. The guy has no sense of right and wrong."

"I used to think he was nice." I hung my head feeling ashamed. How could I've fallen for someone like Star? I looked at Junior, again. How many days had he been sitting on this dock? I slipped the feather behind my ear and asked him, "Want some waffles?"

"I'm starving. Waffles? Where?" He asked.

"Katherine's. It's what's for breakfast today. Katherine always gets up early. Will you come?"

"Are you sure it's ok?" His eyebrows were raised.

"Let's ask." And, with more courage than I usually had, I grabbed Junior's hand and led him back down the dock towards the Wilson house.

Over early-morning waffles, long before the children were up; Will, Katherine, Junior and I sat at the breakfast table and talked like adults do. I found out a lot more about Junior. Will and Katherine knew all the right questions to ask. Junior lived with his parents part-time and on the lake part-time on one of his parents' properties. They paid him for looking after the houses, but he also worked as a fire-dancer.

Now, everyone said, "What?" when Junior said *fire-dancer*, but there really is such a thing, and people get paid for doing it. Junior used words like stage crew, retardant clothing, torches, wands, and special effects. A certain kind of music is played during the whole show. The fire-dancers entertained at campgrounds, conventions, and fairs—all at night, when it was dark. I was speechless. Junior was in show-biz! And to think that some of the Wilson's neighbors thought he was just a beach bum with not much to do.

I kept staring at him while he was explaining all this to Katherine and Will, trying to imagine him twirling fire around his body in figure eights and circles. He turned to me and said, "You'll have to come some time. I bet you'd like it."

"Sure," was all I could say—my eyes as big as they could be and my hands getting sweaty just thinking about it.

Junior said he had to go, and it was Katherine who said, "Ledea, walk him out to the front porch." So, I did. We just kind of looked at each other—knowing more about each other than we ever had before.

"When will you leave?" He asked me.

"Leave, leave what?" I was still imagining him twirling the fire.

"Go home. Back to work. You know, where your mom lives."

"Oh. Tomorrow." And, then, it hit me. Would I ever see Junior again?

"I'll come to visit you if that is ok." Junior said like he could read my mind.

"Visit. Yea. That would be nice." What a relief, I thought. "Do you know where I live?"

"No. But I'll check with Katherine. Or, do you have a phone?"

"Yea. But, guess I don't know the number. No one has asked for it before."

"Ok. I'll check with Katherine. Next week?"

"Next week? You'll check with her then?"

"No. Can I visit then—next week, that is?"

I just nodded my head in the up-and-down way.

We could hear Kyle and Kendra getting up, wanting waffles, wondering where I was.

"You look really beautiful with the feather, Ledea, like a real Lake Princess." He smiled at me real sweet. And before I could even say thanks, he left. Out the door and down the path. I watched him until I could see him no more--a part of me wanting to be just with him. I took the feather from my hair and pressed it to my heart. Junior understood the Lake Princess part of me. I loved him for that.

Katherine returned me the next day to Grandma and Grandpa's house. Before getting out of the car, I turned to tell her how great it had been, but before I could say anything, she looked at me with this very serious look. I knew something was wrong. Had I missed something? Had I done something wrong? Was I being too friendly with Junior?

"Ledea, you remember what Junior said about being careful?"

"You mean, because of Star?"

"Yes, that's what I mean. Well, I'm saying it, too. Be careful where you go; be careful who you let into your house. I really don't think Star was in that fire. I think he's still out there. I'm not trying to scare you; I just want you to be careful."

"What if he does come?" I was starting to get a little worried.

"If he comes to the house, don't let him in. Just call the police. If he shows up at work, call the police. I think there's a warrant out for his arrest. So if you see any sign of him, just call the police. Got that?" I shook my head and kept shaking it when she said, "And, oh, Ledea, please lock all your doors at night and even during the day might be a good idea."

Katherine's words scared me, but the feeling soon went away. Telling Mel about my weekend, talking about Junior being a fire-dancer, taking a warm bath made all those thoughts go away. I looked in the mirror above Grandma and Grandpa's dresser that night, pulled my hair back in a pony tail, and stuck the pheasant feather in it. I danced on the soft carpet in a way I imagined Indian girls dancing when they were oh so happy. I even imagined me dressed as the Lake Princess and helping Junior during his fire dancing shows. I could get a costume to go with my feather.

A knock at the door stopped everything. Mel pushed the door open and peeked in.

"What's all the racket up here?" she asked and looked around snooping.

"Racket?"

"Yea, am I missin' out on a party up here? You're makin' a lot of noise, Ledea. Thought you might be havin' a party."

"No. No party. Just happy, Mel." I sat on the edge of the cushy bed and took the Indian feather out being a little embarrassed even though Mel was my mom.

Mel smiled at me like she was happy for me and, maybe, happy for herself, too.

Pastor Simmons

The following Sunday Mel and I were in the choir singing, "We are one in the Spirit; we are one in the Lord…" Yes, I did join the choir. Alto. The director told me I had a decent voice and to just follow along with the other altos. I looked over the congregation as we sang. "We are *one* in the Spirit; we are *one* in the Lord…" And, I stopped singing thinking about the *one in the spirit*. Our old neighborhood showed up inside my head and then the new one. Marta, next to me, elbowed me and pointed to where we were—like I had gotten lost. But, really I was just thinking. This *one in the spirit* stuff. So, when the choir was done, I circled the name of the song in my bulletin.

Pastor Simmons' sermon was "I Am Only One." He talked about John the Baptist being in the wilderness all by himself. God sent him there, I guess. Anyway, John told everyone to repent. He wasn't thinking about himself, but about Jesus. Pastor Simmons went on to say that although each of us is only one, we should not minimize what God can do through us. Minimize means *make little.* Pastor Simmons reminded us that we may not be like Bach composing great church music or maybe we're not a big-time preacher like Billy Graham from TV, but we can be one of thousands in towns and churches-- more than we can count-- who by their love of God have been lights to their neighbors in quiet ways.

"Has anyone here reached out to the discouraged or needy?" He asked all of us. "Have any of you welcomed into our congregation people who were afraid to come?" He stopped for a while to give us time to think. "Have you prayed for others?" He looked around. People were really quiet. No babies crying or children kicking pews. "In our own way we are to prepare the way for our Lord. A kindness shown when it was not expected, a word of warm welcome—these may be the very paths God will use to enter the life of someone who has not seriously known him. Become a messenger."

When we left church, Pastor Simmons shook our hands like always. "Are you reading James?" He asked me.

"Sort of, Pastor." I had been pretty busy, but I guess a person should never be too busy to spend time with God's word. To be honest with you, I was just being lazy.

"Well, keep at it, Ledea. It's a good book."

That day, Mel and I had pot roast and apple crisp for dinner. We were having fun learning to be better cooks in Grandma's kitchen. After eating, we walked to the senior citizen home to visit Grandma and Grandpa. Grandpa always asked about the car—are we taking good care of it? *Still sittin' in the garage, Dad, hasn't moved a bit,* Mel told him. Grandma always asked about her flowers and the birds—are we feeding them? They soon grew tired and we walked home.

Generally, Mel and I thought life was pretty good—in fact better than it had been for a long time for Mel. And for me, not counting the time I lived with Katherine, it was the best. Junior called every Wednesday right at 7 p.m.—just to check on me, he said. He came to town every other weekend—just to check on me, he said. Being Mrs. Star Johnson kind of bothered me, even though I hadn't seen Star for weeks. I thought of Junior as my friend, you know, not like a boyfriend. At least, that is what I tried to do. Mel helped me out with that one saying people would be talking so I better be careful.

When Junior called during one week, he asked me to go the Clay County Fair with him. He was going to perform as a fire-dancer with his group and would I come and watch and help out? I almost screamed I was so excited, but then this tiny little voice—being Mel's this time—reminded me that I was Mrs. Star Johnson and people would be talking. I didn't want that. So, not being able to explain that to Junior, I just told him "No," kind of sad like.

"That's ok, Ledea," is all he said—like he understood. "Someday. I'll tell you all about it when I get back." It made me like him even more.

I went up to the reading room outside our bedrooms, picked up my Bible and turned to James. Chapter 1, verses 12 and following helped me feel better. I finished the whole book. It's not very long. Maybe that's why Pastor Simmons likes James so much—it's an easy read. There's stuff about resisting the devil, doing good in the world, not swearing, and confessing our sins. Or maybe Pastor Simmons likes James because it covers so much stuff in a few pages. You should read it.

Grandma

One day I was home alone as Mel was at work, and I had a day off. Rainy day, all day, thunder, lightning, the whole works. I watched some of the soaps that Maria and I used to watch. Not a lot had happened. Being a little bored, I started poking around in places I had never snooped. A drawer here, a cupboard there, and ended up in the "box" room as I called it. Remember the extra bedroom with all the boxes? Well, that's where I went.

I followed the path around the boxes that led to the window and pulled the dusty shade to let the light in. There was a window seat covered with a coat of dust and some books about Abraham Lincoln stacked in one corner beside an old black flashlight. I pushed the button forward; it still worked. Putting the flashlight back by the books, I sat down and checked things out. Smelling stuffy and dusty, I opened the window a crack to let in a little fresh air. Looking back into the room, I noticed the boxes were all labeled. Some had dates on them. There were several boxes labeled "tax info." More boxes had "family records" printed neatly. In another stack, there were three boxes for "Christmas decorations," and a box just for "extra tablecloths." Grandma has way too much stuff, I told myself. In one corner were boxes with people's names: Melanie, Mark, Mary. I soon realized that Melanie was Mel, my mom, and that the other two boxes were about Mel's sister, Mary, and her brother, Mark. Pulling the lid off the Mary box, I discovered pictures of Mary as a high school cheerleader, student council president and more—stuff like honor-roll awards and 4-H ribbons. Gosh—Mary had been beautiful, I thought, and popular, too. I stuffed everything back into the box and pushed the cover down—trying to squish everything into place. Mark's box was just as full. I flipped through pictures showing Mark as a football player, basketball player, and awards for all-conference sports stuff. He had attended some leadership summer camp, and there was a picture with about 50 other high school boys dressed in suits and ties. Again, I squished everything back in the box and sat on the lid to make everything fit.

I was getting excited; Mel was next. She never talked much about her past; maybe, I would find out something really interesting about my mom. Pulling the box off the shelf, I noticed right away that it was light compared to the other two boxes. Lifting the lid, I saw a few things at the bottom of the box. One, was a picture of Mel in a brownie outfit—looking kind of sad, I thought. She must have been nine or ten. Another picture showed her as the oldest in a family picture with her parents and Mark and Mary. They were all dressed up. Mark and Mary were seated on their parents' laps. Mel was standing behind all of them a little off to the side. She was not looking at the camera—instead, her eyes looked down. She was dressed in a plaid skirt and nice sweater—her hair pulled back in a pony tail. She was not as pretty as Mary. In fact, she looked very plain.

I picked up another pack of stuff with an old rubber band holding it together that broke when I tried to take it off. They were report cards from first through 11th grade. I only looked at a few. Things like, "improvement needed, lazy, not trying, too many absences, assignments missing, and low test scores" all made me feel really bad so I started pushing everything back into the box. That's when I saw it—a picture of Mel holding a baby. Mel looked to be about 17—real young. She was down on her knees in front of a Christmas tree holding this kind of skinny baby. *It had to be me!* I was dressed in a red-plaid dress with a big bow that almost covered my little pale face. Mel was holding me under my arms like *stand-up baby, stand-up-baby,* but my legs were pretty limp. I can't explain it, but I felt very sad seeing that picture. So sad, that a huge ache found a spot in my chest and just settled there. I put everything back in Mel's box, put on the lid and wanted to cry. This time, I wanted to cry for Mel just thinking what it would be like to take care of a baby when you're so young and when you're someone like Mel.

I was getting a little tired, and the dust was giving me a nose itch, but I kept snooping. There was a bookshelf in another corner. All the books had cloth for covers and were labeled "journal" and had a year on them. I figured that Grandma had kept a diary for most of her life. I pulled out a journal, blew the dust off the top, and opened it. The pages were yellow and the ink was faded. Grandma must have been 17or 18. There was stuff about her going away to Chicago to work as a housekeeper for a family, and then being brought back home because her father was worried about her becoming "too worldly" during the "roaring twenties." Her own mother could not look at her when she came home, and she wondered why. Later, she found out that her father had arranged a marriage for her to a widowed farmer. This farmer turned out to be a wife-beater and an alcoholic. Her parents took her back home, but she was already pregnant. With *my* mom? I wondered.

It was too much for me to think about. At this point, I didn't even want to know how she meant Grandpa and how it all worked out—or did it? My mind was too full. I pushed the journals back into place, left the box room, and returned to my own room. With dusty fingers, I brushed the tears away, climbed into bed and tried to not think about anything from the box room. Questions like, *Ledea, why did you go in there? Ledea, why did you snoop? Ledea, what good does it do to know any of this?* kept my mind hard at work when I wanted to just fall asleep. I tried counting sheep and if you have ever done that, you know how boring it is making my head feel even worse.

The next Sunday when we visited Grandma and Grandpa, I saw Grandma differently. I tried to imagine her being young, her own mother feeling so bad she could not even look at her, and having a father who set up a marriage to someone she did not even know. I wanted to ask her questions. Would she even remember? It made me think about my own life. Would it get better? Would it get worse? Things would change; I knew that. They always did.

We slowly walked Grandpa and Grandma down for afternoon tea and cookies at the home. While eating our cookies, I got brave.

"Grandma, how did you and Grandpa meet?"

"Who?" Bits and pieces of the cookie were dropping from Grandma's mouth, and I noticed a few whiskers I had never noticed before. Some on her chin; some on her upper lip.

"Grandpa? How did you meet him?"

She turned and looked at Grandpa who was making slurpy noises while drinking his tea.

"Can't remember the details. Let's just say that he came along just at the right time." And, she smiled at that as if she remembered. Now, Grandma hardly ever smiled so her answer was ok with me. I had enough problems of my own without finding out about Mel's or

Grandma's and Grandpa's.   I didn't go to the box room again—at least not to snoop.

Star

Whether it be morning, whether it be night,
Whether there be sunlight, or shadows of the dark,
Anytime you seek the Lord, You shall always find,
Anywhere you live, Know that he is there.

Being in choir was a real blessing.   In other words—I loved it.   And, this was one of my favorite songs. After practicing and practicing, I even knew it by heart. With the choir folder pressed to my chest, I sang it out as I looked over the congregation that Sunday kind of swaying back and forth like you do when you have the beat.

Whether there be sorrow, whether there be need,
Whether there be gladness, happiness so sweet,
Any time you seek the Lord, you will always find,

My gaze went to the back of the church and as we finished, *Anywhere you go, Know that He is there,* I saw him. Star! In church? Impossible, I thought. Star said he was egg-nostic. And although I couldn't remember the meaning, I did remember that it meant he wasn't about to show up in any church. Unless....

The choir returned to the choir loft, me looking over my shoulder the whole way trying to get a better view of Star. Even though Mel and I didn't sit together, I walked on other people's shoes to get to her, my robe in their faces all the way.

"Mel!" I said, too loud.

"Ssssh...Ssssh." The others around us got loud, too, all because of me.

"Mel, Star is in church!"

"Star? Where?" Mel started to stand. I hand to pull her down. We were bringing a lot of attention to the choir loft, and it was all my fault.

"In the very back row. Dressed in his usual stuff. Even the cowboy hat." I tried to whisper, but I was nervous, and I think it came out loud.

"NO!" Was all she said while looking and sitting on the edge of the church bench.

"Sssssh." The other members of the choir used to like us. After today, it might change.

"Yes, I saw him," I repeated, took a deep breath, grabbed her robe sleeve in my fist and stared at the back of Pastor Simmons who by this time was blocking my total view of the back of the church.

"NO!" She said it again.

"Ssssh!" I said it this time.

After the sermon about who knows what—how could I concentrate on anything?—Pastor Simmons sat down. I looked sideways to get a view of the back of the church. Star was gone.

"He's not there." Mel elbowed me.

"I know," I answered her.

"Are you sure it was him?" She whispered during The Lord's Prayer. I just hoped God would understand.

And that's the way it was all the way home, *Are you sure it was him?* Over and over until I did say, "No, I'm not sure." But, I knew I was. There was no one like Star.

Mel and I had TV dinners for lunch after church. She had spaghetti with mushrooms, and I had tuna casserole with a crunchy top. Eating in front of the TV, we watched some old western movie. There were outlaws riding into town on their horses and shooting up everything in site. Women and children ran. The sheriff and his deputies were getting their guns ready behind locked doors and on the rooftops. It reminded me that I had not called the police. Remembering what Katherine had said, "If you see any sign of him, just call the police. Got that?"

"Mel!" I turned to her. She was napping on the couch.

"What is it, Ledea?" She kept her eyes shut.

"We need to call the cops?"

"Why? Something wrong?"

"Star. I saw him. Katherine told me ….."

"Ledea, you thought you saw him. But, he couldn't have been there. Woulda' stuck out like a sore thumb. Can't believe he would show up at church."

"But, Mom, I know Star. He *was* there." Although I had been nervous since church, Mel was relaxed enough to sleep which meant she had not really believed he was in the back of the church.

"What am I supposed to do?" I asked her.

"Do? What do you want to do Ledea?"

"Katherine said…." I started again.

"Katherine's not here. You can call the cops but what are you goin' tell them?" This time, Mel sat up and faced me.

"That I saw him—in church," I answered her.

"Ledea, you do what you think needs to be done. I didn't see him so I can't say I did."

At this point, I did start to question myself. Was I imagining this? Did someone who looked a little bit like Star sit in the back of the church? The cowboy hat could have been a shadow cast over someone's head. Mel was snoring by this time. I cleaned up our lunch stuff and saw the garbage was full. Putting a twisty tie on the bag, I carried it to the back door and headed for the garage where we kept it until garbage day. As soon as I opened the side door of the garage, I knew something was missing. There was a big empty space. The car.

Dropping the bag and running back into the house, I tripped on my own feet and fell forward on the sidewalk cutting my lip. I knew why people cursed, and a bad word came to mind, but instead I said, "fudge!" I had heard Katherine use this word when something happened that she wished had not. Mel was still asleep on the couch, so I made up my mind to call Grandpa about the car. It took him a while to get to the phone.

"Grandpa, this is Ledea. How are you today?" I was trying to stay calm.

"Who?" He asked. I had never called him before. He probably was confused.

"Your grand daughter. Mel's girl. I live in your house now. Remember?"

"Oh, yea. Mel's girl. Want to talk to your grandmother? She's right here."

"No. Wait. Grandpa, I need to talk to you." It felt weird calling him Grandpa when I'd rarely talked to him my whole life.

"Sure." I could hear him breathing hard. Every breath was work for him.

"Your car. Do you have it?"

"Course not. Can't drive anymore."

"It's not here." I hoped he wouldn't be mad. Like we hadn't taken care of it.

"Maybe not. Gave my extra keys to Wilbur. Wilbur Kleckner. Told him to take it for a drive. Just in case he wanted to buy it. Maybe he did." Grandpa was getting tired just talking to me. I felt bad for wearing him out.

"Maybe he did, Grandpa. Just checking." I didn't know what else to say. "Say hi to Grandma."

"Sure. Sure thing." And he hung up. I got some ice out of the refrigerator and a wash cloth for my lip. Mel still slept. I could tell this was going to be a very long day.

Mel and I heated up frozen pizzas for supper and played one of the board games from Grandpa and

Grandma's game drawer. Sequence, it was. Pick out a card and put a plastic coin down; over and over, trying to get five in a row while the Grandfather clock tick-tocked loudly in the corner. Mel didn't bring up Star and neither did I. I didn't even mention the car; Grandpa said he had given the keys to someone. So, what could I say? Mel did ask about my lip.

"Fell down. Taking the garbage out. To the garage." I said garage louder just in case she wanted to ask any questions about being in the garage, but she didn't.

"Better be careful, Ledea. Looks nasty. You need to be more careful."

"Yea. I know, Mel." And then I saw it, a sequence. I had two of them, so I won the game. I couldn't even get excited about winning. My lip hurt and I was worried — not really even knowing how to worry or what to worry about. It was just a feeling I had — that something was not right. That something bad was going to happen.

"It's early, but we both work tomorrow. Best get to bed." Mel said. We I put everything back in the box. I checked all the doors to make sure they were locked while Mel turned off the lights downstairs. We said our good nights and headed to our bedrooms. I took a bath with lots of bubbles and put on one of Grandma's nightgowns. It was big on me; me being skinny and all. I felt like I was swimming inside of it. But, when I wrapped it around me, it was warm. I crawled into bed and turned off the light on the stand by the bed. I was not sleepy. Have you ever gone to bed at night and it was totally dark, and there you are with eyes open as big as ever. That was me. A little spooky if you stop and think about it. Big eyes. Dark room. Nothing to see.

Not being able to sleep, I had to think of something to think about. Remembering that Junior was at the fair, I imagined myself there—watching and helping out. It was dark. The fire-dancers always did their act in the dark. I imagined Junior dressed in that retardant costume stuff twirling his figure eights and moving to the music. I was sitting at the foot of the stage surrounded by hundreds of people. Many of them were saying things, like, "Ooooh, ahhhh…," as I dreamed half asleep and half awake. Everyone was making a big deal about how amazing it was. Then, there was more talk.

"For heaven's sake!" and more "oooh's and ahhhh's," except this time not in an amazing way, but kind of angry way.

I sat up in bed and pushed the covers back. I was no longer hearing talk about Junior and the fire-dancers. Someone else had come into my imagination. Or was it real? The sounds were close, but far away, too. I wrapped Grandma's gown tightly around me and headed into the hallway. The sounds were coming from the box room. I quietly opened the door, looked around and followed the sounds to the window I had left open a crack. Peeking below, I saw two figures on the sidewalk trying to get into our basement door.

"For heaven's sake, Betsy," the voice said again, "Get your big butt out of my way. Told you to stay in the car. You're goin' gum up the works. Now, git back there and stay put."

"Butttt.....," a female voice said.

"But, yourself..." Star answered angry-like. "You're settin' my teeth on edge, and I've got to settle an old score. Now, git scarce, woman."

I followed Betsy's big, blond hair walk off into the night and then turned to watch Star fiddle with the lock on the basement door. I almost cried out, "Star, what are you doing?" But then my heart started taking off and telling me to run or do something, anything—and then me starting to remember what Junior, Katherine and everyone had said to do if I saw Star. CALL THE POLICE!

Phone? Phone. Downstairs. Should I wake up Mel or go downstairs to the phone? If Star broke in, would he go in the basement or up the few steps into the kitchen where the only phone hung on the wall? Because I couldn't decide what to do and because my heart was saying "run" when I had no place to go, I stayed. Now, you might have done something different, but there I was in the box room standing by the window just watching Star break into our house. Then, a part of me took over, the subconscious, I think they call it: I picked up that black flashlight sitting by the Abraham Lincoln books as I heard Star pick at our lock. I shined it on the neighbor's windows—turning it off and on, off and on, off and on—like an SOS. Pretty soon, their bedroom lights come on and someone comes to the window. Off and on, off and on—I kept it up with the flashlight. The neighbor, he looks at me, and then he looks at Star bent over the door in that big black cowboy hat. And there right in front of me, this guy in his PJs, grabs the phone and starts talking to someone. I prayed it would be the cops.

I jumped when I heard the siren. Really loud, it was. They caught Star as he was stepping into our house. Flood lights and all. He stuck his hands up right away; didn't even try to run which kind of surprised me. Star had gotten away with so much for so long, I thought he would at least run. Maybe, those cowboy boots were not good for running. He didn't even say anything. Star, with his way with words and all had nothing to say. Simply hung his head and let him put the handcuffs on. I jumped again when someone knocked on the front door—loud! I heard Mel downstairs asking, "What's the problem, officer?" She had slept through everything.

The Ending

You've read those stories that begin, *Once upon a time…* the kind of stories that usually end with, *They lived happily ever after*. This is not that kind of story. Star went off to prison—although not right away—he was held in the county jail during the trial. There were headlines in our newspaper—one of them, "Star not a Star." I read that Star and Stanley Johnson were the same person, and here I was married to him and not really knowing it. As I read this article and others about Star I realized that I fell in love with the guy who came to the Red Owl for chicken. I didn't even really know much about the other Star. It all made me feel kind of embarrassed—embarrassed to not know who I was really married to and embarrassed that he was my husband. Katherine was good to talk to about this. She seemed to understand this better than me—saying that sometimes relationships were difficult—even messy, but that we could always learn something from any experience we had. She prayed with me right at her kitchen table asking God for guidance and thanking him for his everlasting grace which she said everyone needed to live and on a daily basis.

Pastor Simmons visited Mel and me often during the trial period. He always walked in with a plate of homemade chocolate chip cookies in one hand and a Bible under his arm.

"Ledea, I've been talking to you about James. Where's that Bible you've been reading?" I went up to my bedroom and got it off my bed stand. "Turn to James, Chapter 1. Find verses 5-6 and read—out loud."

Thumbing through the New Testament while Pastor Simmons took his third chocolate chip cookie... Matthew, Mark, Luke, James... I found it. I started reading it to myself when he interrupted me, "Out loud, Ledea. We all need to hear this."

"If any of you lacks wisdom, he should pray to God, who will give it to him; because God gives generously and graciously to all. But when you pray, you must believe and not doubt at all." I looked up. He was staring at me real hard.

"Good, good, good," Pastor Simmons said with two fingers rubbing his whiskery chin. "Read it again." And, I did. Mel kind of rolled her eyes, but she was listening.

"What do you think that means, Ledea, for you?" Pastor Simmons brushed his cookie-crumbed hands on his pants and looked at the ceiling as if he had to think about it, too.

"Well," I wasn't a preacher and couldn't answer it the way a preacher would. I looked at the verse, again, reading it to myself. Mel and Pastor Simmons sat quietly, although I did hear Mel clear her throat once or twice probably because she was nervous, and she was trying to get me talking so she wouldn't have to say anything.

"I think God is telling me that because I don't know what to do right now—or even how to think-- about all this stuff with Star and our marriage, that I need to pray about it, and then believe that God will help me understand it all and show me how to take care of things. You preached once about the lillies of the field and how God takes care of those, so he will take care of us. Right? No matter what. Right? I just need to be more thankful for all that he does. I guess a lot of stuff he's taken care of without me even asking. I could have burned in the fire at the little brown house, I could have drowned—thanks to Betsy. I met Katherine. I discovered the Lake Princess...." I was rattling on and on like no one was listening when I realized I had mentioned "Lake Princess"—

"Lake Princess?" both Pastor Simmons and Mel said at the same time.

"Yes, she's….someone….who… Well, never mind. She's a good person and I'll tell you about her some other time." With that, I grabbed the cookie plate, started eating one and passed the plate around the table.

Pastor Simmons cleared his throat. "You seem to understand the verse from James, Ledea. Good for you. This is not an easy time for any of you. Prayer can move mountains as they say. We don't have a mountain, here, but we do have a troublesome anthill—bothersome it is. But things will work out so that you can go on with your life, I'm sure."

"But, I am *married* to Star," I pretty much spat out seeing cookie crumbs on the table in front of me, and I noticed one got stuck in Pastor Simmons' whiskers. But, there were no two ways about it. I was Mrs. Star Johnson or Mrs. Stanley Johnson. I had signed a certificate at the court house making me Star's wife. Rubbing his whiskers, again, and discovering the cookie crumb, Pastor Simmons picked up a napkin. I was hoping he thought the cookie crumb was his and not mine.

"Yes, Ledea, you are." He shook his head sad-like—like he couldn't believe it—or he didn't know what to do about it. "Bothersome," he used the word again.

"Bothersome," this time it came from Mel with her shaking her head, too.

"Look, I made a mistake," I whined. "And I don't know what to do." With that I ran out of the house acting like the child I no longer was. Going out to Grandpa's now-empty garage, I sat on the cold cement floor and cried a bucket of tears. For a time, I had felt so special being Star's wife—being wanted, being loved, being a part of someone's life. Now, I was the wife of a jailbird. I felt stupid, lonely, and very sad, and so I cried another bucket load of tears until I was nothing but a mess of bones and skin on that garage floor.

I must have fallen asleep, because I woke up with a huge headache and the shivers. Sitting up, I looked out the garage window to see darkness. Standing up, I went to the door, turned the knob and started to walk to the house—my bones feeling all stiff and crackly. There in the dark were Mel and Pastor Simmons sitting in lawn chairs like lawn statues.

"It's about time," Mel said quiet-like, not mad at all.

"Good night, Ledea. See you tomorrow," Pastor Simmons added as he quietly walked to his car—empty cookie plate and Bible in hand.

Climbing into bed that night, a little glimmer of hope showed up in my head. It was the picture of Pastor Simmons and Mel in lawn chairs that started it. Next, I thought of Katherine and her family. Then, the choir members at church. And, next all the people at the Red Owl who smiled and greeted me whenever I showed up. Those people would all still be there for me. And, so I thanked God for them and fell asleep feeling better.

Ledea

Life changed for me and I guess it was for the better. Star didn't call but maybe he wasn't allowed being in prison and all. He could have written. Something like—*Ledea, I'm sorry I messed up your life. I still love you.*—would have worked. But, at the same time, I didn't know if I really wanted Star to love me. He was so bad. I wanted good. And, for that reason, at least to start out with, I didn't write Star either or try to call or even visit.

Junior still called once a week. We'd talk for about 20 minutes or more before Mel would yell, "Whatcha talkin' about, anyway?" and sit out in the kitchen just listening to what I had to say because she had nothing else to do. There was no lovey-dovey stuff although I always felt kind of nice inside just talking to him. No, Junior would talk about his fire dancing stuff. Where he was going. The music and the outfits. Stuff like that. *One day you'll be able to go with me* is what he said to me one night on the phone. And then he said, *Ledea, are you still there?* because I was speechless just thinking about him telling me that.

"Yes, I'm here." I finally said.

"Good. I'm glad you are," was his answer. And then he said, "Goodbye" real quiet like. I hung up the phone and Mel said, "Ledea, cat got your tongue?" and the spell was broken because her words reminded me of Star's. You see I wanted to hate Star because I felt he had pretty much ruined my life; not that I had much of one when he met me. But, I had possibilities like everyone else. If Star had never paid attention to me at the Red Owl. If I had read the paper on my own and gotten that job at Katherine's. If I had met Junior on my own while working at Katherine's. Who knows. If, if, if.... If's were going to get me no where. So I reminded myself real often of the Bible verse Pastor Simmons told me about asking for wisdom from God and tried to do my best.

Katherine called at least once a week, too. Mel complained about the phone bill but I wasn't doing the calling; I had to remind her of that. I kind of thought that Mel was jealous. No one called her except for Pastor Simmons asking *is it ok if I come?* And *How's it goin'*?

Pastor Simmons not only helped me during his many visits but his sermons every Sunday seemed to be planned just for me. One Sunday the sermon was "Dealing with Burdens." He talked about how it is heartbreaking to put your faith in someone and, then, be big-timed disappointed. When that happens we can't just expect God to drop down from heaven and fix it for us. There may be burdens that others can't fix for us or that God chooses not to fix for us. Nevertheless (Pastor Simmons always rolls this off his tongue), God wants us to turn it over to him. Let it go. *Let go and let God.* I think those were his exact words.

On another Sunday Pastor talked about SERVICE and how it is the way to FREEDOM. Now, you may be thinking—*Ledea is free of Star, what more does she want?* But, to be real honest, I was not feeling free at all. I was feeling the burden he talked about earlier. Pastor

218

Simmons explained that one way to feel free is to GIVE. We can give by helping others in any way we can. Maybe it's a smile to someone who needs one. Offering to help out with Sunday School. Singing in the choir. Reading to a shut-in. Taking flowers to a neighbor with a new baby. And, you know what, it worked. I tried to plan a *giving* thing each and every day and I began to feel free. Plus, when I was thinking about others, I wasn't thinking about Star or myself.

One day, Mel and I went together and bought a few daisies. We took them to our neighbor lady who never gets out. You should have seen the smile on her face when we came to the door holding that colorful bouquet. On another day, I invited the neighbor behind the alley over for coffee. His wife was already dead. He walked over with his cane. I could tell he had cleaned up some because his bald head was shiny, and he smelled a little like he had put on some cologne or at least deodorant. Mel talked more that day than she had in a long time. I also began looking for little ways I could be a better worker at the Red Owl. You'd be surprised what you can find to do extra when you start looking.

Pastor Simmons explained that God treats us with a love that has no limits no matter who we are or what we have done. So, our goal should be to do to others not only as we wish others would do to us (like the Golden Rule says), but as God has actually done to us. Because of this, I started thinking about Star, again. I wasn't the kind of person to try to get even—it wasn't part of my personality, like Mel told me. However, after thinking about all of this, I knew I would have to forgive Star and focus on God's purpose for my life if I wanted to get rid of the burden and feel the kind of *free* God was talking about. This would be work.

Pastor Simmons helped me work through all of this and Mel and me both learned a lot. Pastor Simmons challenged me one day.

"Ledea, you been reading James?" He always asked me that. I wanted to say, "Yea, yea, yea..." as soon as he started with the, "Ledea, you been reading..." But I had manners and I knew this would be disrespectful even though Mel and I had gotten pretty close to Pastor Simmons. All those visits with chocolate chip cookies caused it. So, I just politely answered.

"Yes, Pastor Simmons, I have."

"Then, it's time to get on with it."

"What?" *Get-on-with-what?* I thought.

"Get on with it." He repeated. I wasn't hard of hearing.

"What?" He was smiling because sometimes he liked to confuse me.

"What about Matthew, Mark, and Luke?"

"Uh... What about them?" I asked.

"Well, those books are just waiting for you to dig in."

"They are?" I smiled and frowned at the same time. The Bible was a huge book. Did Pastor Simmons expect me to read the whole thing?

"Ledea," he said quietly. "You do not have to be a scholar to read the Bible. You simply need to read it. Prayerfully. God will take care of the rest."

"Oh. Wow. It's a big book." I didn't say wow like "wow!" I just said it like a regular word, because I was already worn-out just thinking about reading the whole Bible.

"Well, in a sense it's God's love letter to you. So, it's worth reading. A little every day and it won't seem like such a huge task."

"OK," is all I said. I was thinking about the love letter part and how if I ever got one, I would want to read it over and over—even memorize certain parts. When the word *memorize* came up in my mind, I remembered memorizing some of my favorite verses when I was a child—even putting them under my pillow like a treasure. Pastor Simmons interrupted my thoughts, but he must have known a little about mind-reading with what he said. After-all he is a man of God. Because this is what he said…

"Remember, when you were but a child coming up to children's sermons? Been a few years, hasn't it? I remember a little girl who would memorize her favorite verses. You were very good at it."

I was shaking my head like *how did you know that was what I was thinking about, too?*

"Ledea, do you remember any of those verses?"

Within a few moments, some of them came flooding back even though I had not thought about it for along time.

"The Lord is my helper. I will not be afraid. What can man do to me?"

"From Hebrews, that one is…" Pastor filled in.

"And," I interrupted him, because my memory was working real good…"The eternal God is your dwelling place and underneath are the everlasting arms." I spoke clearly. Mel's eyebrows were up in the air. Had she forgotten how I loved to do this?

"A word fitly spoken is like apples of gold in pictures of silver," I continued.

"Oh, yes, Proverbs," Pastor Simmons replied. I think he was impressed.

Then, I bowed my head. I guess I felt bad for not thinking about all of this for so long. And, I think I felt something Pastor Simmons calls grace. It's a God-like thing. Katherine used to say that everyone needed it; you can't live without it. And, because I was feeling this way, I remembered the most wow verse of all. The one about a **secret** from Colossians. With my head still down, I stated it quietly, "…the secret is that Christ is in you."

All Pastor Simmons said was, "Thank you, Ledea. Let's close our little visit today with The Lord's Prayer."

Although I had been saying it for years, it took on more meaning than it ever had before. Pastor Simmons started it but Mel, me and Pastor prayed it together.

Our Father, who art in heaven, hallowed be thy name.

Thy kingdom come, thy will be done on Earth as it is in Heaven.

(It is important to get things done, here..on earth, God is telling us.)

Give us this day our daily bread.

And forgive us our trespasses as we forgive those who trespass against us.

(Yes, I could forgive, Star; God, always forgave me.)

And, lead us not into temptation, but deliver us from evil.

....

Quietly, we said "amen" and just sat there listening to the clock ticking and a bird or two in the branches outside Grandma and Grandpa's house.

Pastor Simmons broke the quiet spell with.... "Back then, you had a child-like faith—a wonderful thing—something God tells us we need to have even as adults. However, God also wants us to grow-up in our faith, too. You have what you need; you just need to continue on with the journey—it's a faith journey—a walk we all need to take."

He didn't even say goodbye that day. Just picked up his Bible and walked slowly toward the door kind of tired-like. I saw the cookie plate was still on the coffee table with all the cookies left. I think he left it on purpose so I didn't call him back in.

From that day on, my insides were a little lighter. I think I smiled more. Mel and I went back and forth to work, but at the same time, we paid more attention to the people around us. What did they need? Someone to talk to? A "good morning?" Some help with errands?

I sent a small Bible to Star with a letter explaining some of my feelings and, yes, I did say that I forgave him. As I was wrapping this all up, I remembered that Star could not read. And, so on the outside of the envelope, I wrote, *Please read to Star Johnson.*

I didn't say why. I didn't want Star to feel bad which sort of says something about how I felt about him. If I really believed the verse in the Bible about the secret, I would have to believe that Star had the secret, too. It was just hidden or it wasn't the right time in Star's life for him to be aware of it.

When Star had the letter read to him, this is what he would hear…

Dear Star,

Hi, it's me Ledea. I guess you will remember me even though we have not talked for some time. I don't think I really understand all the bad stuff that happened. Maybe, you do. I hope you can work it out in some way and be a better person for it. I am sending you a Bible.

I took a highlighter and highlighted some of my favorite verses. They're real easy to find. Just look for yellow.

Also, Star, have someone read James for you, especially Chapter 1, verses 2-3.

And, when they get done with that, they can read all of it to you—if they have time.

God loves you,

Ledea

I want to thank you for reading my book. Your life, of course, is not like mine. But, as Pastor Simmons said, we are all on a faith journey. Whether you think you are or not—you are. I know this because God breathed into Adam the breath of life, and, well, if Adam was the first father, you get the picture. You are connected to God whether you have thought about it or not. This is part of the secret. I want to read you the whole verse from Colossians. You might even want to memorize it. It's Colossians 1:27. I'm reading from the Good News New Testament in Today's English Version, so yours might be a little different, but the meaning is the same.

*God's plan is to make known his **secret** to his people, this rich and glorious **secret** which he has for all peoples. And the **secret** is that Christ is in you, which means that you will share in the glory of God.*

Knowing this should make us all want to dance and sing and give praise. Everyone has bad days, but maybe if we would concentrate more on the secret, the bad days wouldn't seem so bad knowing how much God really loves us and that we are all a part of his plan for us.

Pastor Simmons helped me write a prayer for all of us. I hope you like it.

Dearest heavenly Father, you are the God of the universe. You created all things and if we stop and think of this, we are amazed. Your son, Jesus, died on the cross so that we might have eternal life. What a sacrifice. We only have to believe to get this gift. But, you have also called us to let others know of the coming of your kingdom—like it says in the Lord's Prayer—thy kingdom come, they will be done on Earth as it is in Heaven. Give us the courage that we may faithfully live to share your love and peace every day of our lives. We ask this in your holy name. To God be the glory.

Amen and love you,

Ledea

PS—Even though Colossians has the verse about the secret, read James. It's a good start.

CPSIA information can be obtained
at www.ICGtesting.com
Printed in the USA
FFOW01n1844020315
11392FF

9 781603 833226